Without war
over her eyes
husky voice said, close to her ear,
'Guess who?'

Virginia's heart pounding like a trip hammer, her breath coming in shallow gasps, she stared into Ryan's tough, hard-boned face. A face she knew as well as her own. A face she had often looked into while they made love.

He put out a hand, and with a proprietary gesture brushed a loose tendril of curly hair back from her pale cheek.

'My dear Virginia, there's no need to act as if you're afraid of me.'

'So you did catch sight of me in the gallery. Why didn't you say anything?'

Ryan's voice was ironic as he told her, 'I thought I'd surprise you.'

Lee Wilkinson lives with her husband in a three-hundred-year-old stone cottage in a Derbyshire village, which most winters gets cut off by snow. They both enjoy travelling and recently, joining forces with their daughter and son-in-law, spent a year going round the world 'on a shoestring' while their son looked after Kelly, their much loved German shepherd dog. Her hobbies are reading and gardening and holding impromptu barbecues for her long-suffering family and friends.

Recent titles by the same author:

MARRIAGE ON THE AGENDA
WEDDING ON DEMAND
A VENGEFUL DECEPTION

RYAN'S REVENGE

BY
LEE WILKINSON

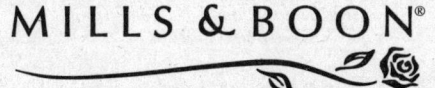

DID YOU PURCHASE THIS BOOK WITHOUT A COVER?
If you did, you should be aware it is **stolen property** as it was reported *unsold and destroyed* by a retailer. Neither the author nor the publisher has received any payment for this book.

All the characters in this book have no existence outside the imagination of the author, and have no relation whatsoever to anyone bearing the same name or names. They are not even distantly inspired by any individual known or unknown to the author, and all the incidents are pure invention.

All Rights Reserved including the right of reproduction in whole or in part in any form. This edition is published by arrangement with Harlequin Enterprises II B.V. The text of this publication or any part thereof may not be reproduced or transmitted in any form or by any means, electronic or mechanical, including photocopying, recording, storage in an information retrieval system, or otherwise, without the written permission of the publisher.

This book is sold subject to the condition that it shall not, by way of trade or otherwise, be lent, resold, hired out or otherwise circulated without the prior consent of the publisher in any form of binding or cover other than that in which it is published and without a similar condition including this condition being imposed on the subsequent purchaser.

MILLS & BOON and MILLS & BOON with the Rose Device are registered trademarks of the publisher.

*First published in Great Britain 2002
Harlequin Mills & Boon Limited,
Eton House, 18-24 Paradise Road, Richmond, Surrey TW9 1SR*

© Lee Wilkinson 2002

ISBN 0 263 82917 0

*Set in Times Roman 10½ on 11¼ pt.
01-0302-49318*

*Printed and bound in Spain
by Litografia Rosés, S.A., Barcelona*

CHAPTER ONE

WARM June sunshine poured in through the open window, a beneficence after the late and miserably cold spring. In nearby Kenelm Park a dog yapped excitedly, shrill above the continuous, muted roar of London's traffic.

Glancing from her second-floor window, Virginia saw between the trees the flash of a bright red ball being thrown, and smiled, before returning to her cataloging.

A moment later the internal phone on her desk rang. Reaching out a slender, long-fingered hand she picked up the receiver. 'Yes?'

Helen's voice said formally, 'Miss Ashley, there's a gentleman here asking if we have any paintings by either Brad or Mia Adams. I've explained that there are none listed, but he'd like to know if we're able to acquire any.'

During the past ten years the Adams' work had become widely sought after, and Virginia had grown used to the idea of her parents being well known—at least in the world of art.

'I'll come down,' she said.

Helen Hutchings, a nice-looking forty-year-old widow, handled casual sales of the good contemporary art that the Charles Raynor Gallery displayed, while Virginia dealt with specialist requests or queries.

Checking that no wisps of silky ash-brown hair had escaped from her neat chignon, and donning the heavy glasses that changed her appearance and made her look considerably older than her twenty-four years, she left her office, slender and business-like in a charcoal-grey silk suit.

The long oval gallery had a balcony running around it and was open to the skylights, where today the oatmeal-coloured blinds were in place because of the bright sunshine.

Peering over the wrought-iron balcony rail, she saw that a few people, mainly tourists she judged, were browsing. At the far end, she caught a glimpse of a tall, well-built man with dark hair who was standing by the reception desk.

His stance was easy, anything but impatient, yet he had an unmistakable air of *waiting*.

As she reached the stairs, which at the bottom were roped off with a crimson and gold tasselled cord that held a notice saying Private, he turned to glance in her direction.

Ryan.

There was no mistaking that lean, hard-boned face, the set of the shoulders, the carriage of that dark head, the strong yet graceful physique.

Though it was much too far away to see the colour of his eyes, she knew quite well that they were midway between dark blue and violet.

Her breath caught in her throat. Virginia stopped dead, gripping the banister rail convulsively.

Even after her flight from New York and her return to London she had been afraid of seeing him, on edge and wary of every tall, dark-haired man who came into sight.

Only over the last six months or so had she started to feel relatively safe, confident that she had left the past behind her.

Now it seemed that her confidence had been premature.

Her heart was beginning to pound and, a rush of adrenalin galvanising her into action, she turned and fled back to the safety of her office.

Sinking down at her desk, her stomach churning sickeningly, she prayed that he hadn't seen and recognised her.

If he *had*, Ryan wasn't the kind of man to walk quietly away. Remembering how he'd said, 'I'll never let you go,' she shuddered.

In spite of all that had been between them she had left

him. Unable to bear the pain of his perfidy, afraid to confront him for fear of what damage it might do to the family, she had run without a word.

He wouldn't easily forgive her for that.

But if he *hadn't* recognised her, the situation could be saved...

Hoping against hope that Charles was back from his early afternoon appointment, she reached for the internal phone.

There was no answer from his office, which was on the ground floor, and she tried the private showroom and then, in mounting desperation, the strongroom.

When, his voice sounding abstracted, he answered, 'Yes... What is it?' Virginia could have wept with relief.

'I'm sorry to disturb you, but could you possibly find time to see a prospective customer who's waiting at reception?'

'What does he or she want?' he queried in his rather dry, precise manner.

'He asked if we can acquire any Adams paintings.'

Sounding surprised, Charles said, 'Surely you can deal with that?'

'It's someone I...once knew, and I'd rather not have to meet again.'

Though Virginia had done her best to play it down, with the perception of a man in love, he picked up the urgency. 'Very well. Leave it to me.'

Fear darkening her grey-green eyes almost to charcoal, she wondered, why, oh, why, out of all the art galleries in London, had Ryan chanced to come into this one?

Since her return to London two-and-a-half years ago, she had used her middle name as a surname and had virtually lived in hiding. No one knew where she was. Not even her parents.

She had been staying in a cheap hotel off the Bayswater

Road and, with very little money and Christmas coming up, had been badly in need of a job.

The employment agency she'd approached had sent her to the Raynor Gallery where she had been interviewed by Charles himself.

She had told him about the course on the practical and administrative side of art she had taken at college, and had explained, without giving any details, that she had just returned from the States.

After studying her thoughtfully while she spoke, he had offered her a post as his assistant.

After she had been working for him for almost a year, the gallery had started to handle the Adams' work, and when Charles had suggested that *she* should be their contact she had been forced to tell him at least part of the truth.

'Virginia, my dear,' he protested, 'as you're their daughter, surely—'

'I don't want them to know where I am.'

They were acquainted with Ryan, and that made any communication with them potentially dangerous.

Charles frowned. 'But won't they worry about you?'

'No, I'm certain they won't. You see we've never been a family in the real sense of the word.'

Seeing he was unconvinced, she explained, 'Mother was fresh out of art school when she met my father, who was over from the States.

'They'd both been painting since they were children, and lived for art. That's probably what drew them together.

'After they married they lived in Greenwich Village for several years before coming back to settle in England. By the time I was born they were well into their thirties.

'I was a mistake. Neither of them wanted me. If mother hadn't been brought up to believe life was sacred, I think she might well have had an abortion.'

'Oh surely not!' Charles, a mild-mannered, conventional man, sounded shocked by her bluntness.

'They were both so wrapped up in their work that a baby was an unlooked-for and unwelcome complication in their lives...'

Though she spoke flatly, dispassionately, he could feel her abiding sense of rejection, and his heart bled for her.

'They were well-off financially, and their solution was a series of nannies, and a girl's boarding school as soon as I was old enough.

'I was on the point of leaving school and starting college when they went back to New York to live.'

'They left you behind?'

'I was nearly eighteen by then.'

'But surely they helped to support you? Financially, I mean?'

'No, I didn't want them to. I preferred to take evening and weekend jobs and stay independent...

'So you see, not knowing where I am now won't worry them in the slightest. In fact I doubt if they ever give me a thought.'

'Very well, if you're sure?'

'I'm quite sure.'

'Then, I'll deal with them personally.'

'You won't say anything?' she asked anxiously.

'Not a word. Your secret's safe with me.'

She felt a rush of affection for him. He was a thoroughly nice man and, knowing that he would keep his promise, she breathed easier.

Until now...

The latch clicked.

She glanced up sharply, her heart in her mouth.

It was Charles, neat and conservative in a lightweight business suit, a lock of fair hair falling over his high forehead giving him a boyish air that belied his forty-three years.

Seeing her face had lost all trace of colour, he said reassuringly, 'There's no need to look so concerned. He's gone.'

Perhaps, subconsciously, she had been half expecting Ryan to come bursting in, and relief was washing over her like a warm tide when a sudden thought made her query anxiously, 'He didn't ask about me?'

Dropping into the chair opposite, Charles raised a fair brow. 'Why should he?'

She worried her lower lip. 'I'd started to go down when I realised who it was. I thought he might have seen and recognised me.'

'He made no mention of it,' Charles assured her calmly. 'And, as he appears to be the type who wouldn't have hesitated to ask about anything he wanted to know, I think we can safely assume he didn't.'

Watching Virginia relax perceptibly, he wondered what had passed between her and the powerful-looking man he'd just been talking to.

From her reactions it was clear that her feelings had been a great deal deeper than her casual 'someone I once knew' had implied. It might even be part of the reason she had refused his offer of marriage...

Hoping for further reassurance that Ryan's visit *had* been just chance, she asked, 'What did he actually say? How did he act?'

'His manner was quite straightforward and purposeful. He told me his name was Ryan Falconer, and that he'd like to acquire, amongst other things, some of the earlier Adams paintings. I promised I'd put out some feelers and let him know the chances as soon as possible...'

'Is he staying in England?'

'For a few days, apparently. As well as his home address in Manhattan, he gave me the phone number of a Mayfair hotel.'

Mayfair. She repressed a shiver. Practically on their doorstep and much too close for comfort.

'Though he's primarily a businessman, a Wall Street investment banker, I understand, he's interested in art and owns the Falconer Gallery in New York... But possibly you knew that?'

'Yes.'

When she failed to elaborate, Charles went on, 'However, I gather the paintings he's hoping to buy are for his private collection. He mentioned one by Mia Adams that he'd particularly like to own, *Wednesday's Child*...'

She froze.

'Falconer believes it was painted seven or eight years ago, and is one of her best. Though I must say I've never heard of it... He made it clear that money's no object, so I've promised to do what I can. Of course, even if I'm able to locate it, the present owner might not be willing to sell.'

Something about Virginia's utter stillness made Charles ask, 'Do *you* remember it by any chance?'

Taking a deep breath, she admitted, 'As a matter of fact I do. I sat for it. I wasn't quite seventeen.'

His light blue eyes glowing with interest, he exclaimed, 'I didn't realise your mother had ever used you as a model!'

'It was just the once. I'd been invited to spend the summer holidays with a school friend—Jane belonged to a big happy family, and I was looking forward to it—but at the last minute the visit had to be cancelled, so I went home.

'Mother said that as I was there she might as well make use of me. I tried hard to do just as she wanted, but for some reason she disliked the finished portrait, and she never asked me to sit again.'

'What did *you* think of it?'

'I didn't see it,' Virginia said flatly. 'She told me that it needed framing, and the next time I went home, it had been sold...'

And now Ryan wanted to buy it.

That fact disturbed her almost as much as seeing him again...

But maybe it was just chance that had made him specify *Wednesday's Child*? Maybe he didn't know that she had been the sitter?

Almost before the thought was completed, a sure and certain instinct told her it was no chance. He *knew* all right.

She shivered.

Watching her face, Charles asked shrewdly, 'If I am able to locate and acquire that particular painting, how do you feel about Falconer having it?'

With careful understatement, she admitted, 'I'd rather he didn't.'

'Then, I'll tell him I had no luck.'

Recalling the problems and financial losses that Charles had suffered over the past year, she swallowed hard and made herself say, 'No, if you *are* able to acquire it and he's willing to pay well, you mustn't let my silly prejudices stand in the way of business.'

'Well, we'll see,' he said noncommittally. 'Things might well be looking up.'

Before she could question that somewhat cryptic statement, he glanced at his watch. 'It's almost four o'clock. I'd best be getting on.'

Rising to his feet, a tall, spare figure with slightly rounded shoulders, he suggested with the solicitude he always displayed for her, 'You're looking a bit peaky, why don't you go home?'

Thoroughly unsettled, her head throbbing dully, and never having felt less like work, she said gratefully, 'I've got a bit of a headache, so I think I will, if you really don't mind?'

Smiling, he shook his head. 'As it's Monday, I'm quite sure Helen and I can deal with anything that may crop up in the next hour or so.'

At the door, he paused to say, 'Oh, by the way, I won't be coming home at the usual time. I've agreed to have dinner with the client I saw earlier this afternoon…'

Her heart sank. Somehow, after what had happened, she needed his comforting, undemanding presence.

'And as it's my turn to cook—' when Virginia had first moved into his spare room, they had reached an amicable arrangement whereby they cooked on alternate evenings '—I suggest you get a takeaway, on me...'

Well aware that his sensitive antennae had picked up her unspoken need, she asked with determined lightness, 'Will you run to a Chinese?'

He grinned. 'I might, if you promise to save me some prawn crackers.'

'Done!'

'I don't expect to be late but, if by any chance I am, don't wait up for me. You look as if you could do with an early night. Oh, and if you're not feeling up to scratch, take a taxi home.'

Charles was so genuinely kind, so caring, Virginia thought as the door closed behind him. He would make a wonderful husband for the right woman.

He was an excellent companion, easy to talk to and good-tempered, with that rarest of gifts, the ability to see another person's point of view.

Added to that, he was a good-looking man with a quiet charm and undeniable sex appeal. Helen, she was almost certain, was in love with him, and had been for the past year.

It was a great pity that *she* couldn't love him in the way he wanted her to.

A few weeks before, as they'd washed the dishes together after their evening meal, he had broached the question of marriage, diffidently, feeling his way, afraid of scaring her off.

Until then she had thought of him as a confirmed bachelor, set in his ways. It had never occurred to her that he might propose, and he'd been skirting round the subject for several minutes before she'd had the faintest inkling of what had been in his mind.

'I hadn't realised how much I lacked companionship until you came along... Since you've been living here...well, it's made a great difference to my life... And you seem happy with the arrangement...?'

'Yes, I am.' She smiled at him warmly.

Bolstered by that smile, his blue eyes serious, he finally came to the point. 'Virginia...there's something I want to ask you... But if the answer's no, promise me it won't make any difference to our friendship...'

'I promise.'

'You must know I love you...'

She had suspected he was getting fond of her, but had regarded it as the kind of affection he might have felt for any close friend.

'Don't you think it might be something to do with propinquity?' she suggested gently.

Shaking his head, he said, 'I've loved you ever since I set eyes on you...' Then formally, he said, 'It would make me very happy if you would agree to marry me.'

Just for an instant she was tempted. It would be lovely to have a husband, a home that was really hers and, sooner or later, children.

Though she liked her chosen career and had worked hard to gain the knowledge and the eye that had put her on the road to success, it had always taken second place to her dream of being part of a close and happy family.

But it wouldn't be fair to Charles to marry him. He deserved a wife who would love him passionately, rather than a woman who felt merely affection for him.

In no doubt of her answer now, she took a deep, steadying breath. 'I'm sorry...more sorry than I can say...but I can't.'

'Is it the age difference?'

'No,' she answered truthfully. If she'd loved him enough age wouldn't have mattered.

He hung the tea towel up carefully, and pushed back the lock of fair hair that fell over his forehead. 'I had hoped, in view of how well we get along, that you might at least consider it. But perhaps you don't like me sufficiently?'

'I both like and respect you, in fact I'm very fond of you, but—'

'Surely that would be enough to make it work?' he broke in, his blue eyes eager.

She half shook her head. 'Fondness isn't enough.'

'I'm prepared to give it a try. A lot of marriages must be based on less.'

'No, it wouldn't be fair to you...'

Seeing the discomfort on her face, he patted her hand and said firmly, 'Don't worry. I promise I won't bring it up again.

'But don't forget I love you. I'd do anything for you... And if you should ever change your mind, the offer's still open.'

He was a wonderful man. A man in a million. She *wanted* to love him. But love was something that could neither be ordered nor controlled.

She knew that to her cost.

Seeing the dangers, she had tried not to love Ryan... Without success.

But she wouldn't think about Ryan.

As though amused by her decision, Ryan's dark face with those blue-violet eyes smiled back at her mockingly.

Her only coherent thought on first meeting him had been that never before had she seen eyes of such a fascinating colour on any other person...

Damn! there she was doing it.

Gritting her teeth, she closed and locked the window, then gathering up her shoulder bag, made her way down the uncarpeted rear stairs and out of the green-painted staff door onto the cobbled street.

Kenelm Mews, with the backs of buildings on one side and the iron railings of Kenelm Park on the other, was filled with slanting sunlight and the summer-in-the-city smell of dust and petrol fumes and melting tarmac.

Instead of turning the corner into the main road and either looking for a taxi or heading for the bus stop, as she usually did when Charles didn't drive her home, she hesitated.

With its sun-dappled flower beds and shady trees Kenelm looked green and pleasant. If she walked home across the park, it might help to clear her head and relax some of the remaining tension.

Suddenly impatient with her glasses, she stuffed them into her bag and set off through wrought-iron gates that stood open invitingly.

Passing the Victorian bandstand, and the velvety smooth bowling greens where sedate cream-clad figures were standing in little groups, Virginia took a path that skirted the small boating lake.

She walked briskly as though trying to outpace her thoughts. But try as she might, they kept returning to Ryan and his reason for coming into the gallery. Why did he want *Wednesday's Child*?

So he had an image of her? Something to metaphorically stick pins into?

The thought of so much pent-up anger and hatred directed towards herself, frightened her half to death. Her legs starting to tremble, she sank down on the nearest bench, staring blindly across the lake.

She had hoped that time would lessen the animosity she guessed he must feel towards her.

But why should it?

Time hadn't lessened the way she felt.

The bewilderment, the sense of betrayal, the resentment, the hurt...

Without warning, hands came over her eyes and a low, slightly husky voice, a voice that would have made her turn back from the gates of heaven, said close to her ear, 'Guess who?'

Her heart seemed to stop beating, robbing her brain of blood and her lungs of oxygen. Faintness washed over her, swirling her into oblivion...

As the mists began to clear, she found herself held securely against a broad chest, her head resting on a muscular shoulder, the sun warm on her face.

Gathering her senses as best she could, she tried to struggle free.

An elderly woman walking past with a liver-and-white spaniel on a lead, gave them a quick, curious glance and, deciding they were lovers, walked on.

When Virginia made a further, more determined, effort, the imprisoning arms fell away, allowing her to sit upright.

Her heart pounding like a trip hammer, her breath coming in shallow gasps, she stared into Ryan's tough, hard-boned face. A face she knew as well as she knew her own. A face she had often looked into while they'd made love.

The thick dark hair that tried to curl was cut fairly short, but by no means the shaven-headed look she so disliked; his chiselled mouth was as beautiful as she remembered, as were those long-lashed eyes, the colour of indigo.

Eyes that would have made the most ordinary man extraordinary. Except, of course, that Ryan was far from ordinary. Even without those remarkable eyes he would have stood out in a crowd...

He put out a hand, and with a proprietary gesture brushed a loose tendril of brown curly hair back from her pale cheek.

She flinched away as though he'd struck her.

His expression pained, he protested, 'My dear Virginia, there's no need to act as if you're afraid of me.'

'So you did catch sight of me in the gallery,' she said hoarsely.

'Just a glimpse before you bolted. Running away seems to be your forte.'

Biting her lip, she asked, 'Why didn't you say anything to Charles?'

His voice ironic, he told her, 'I thought I'd surprise you.'

He'd certainly succeeded in doing that. Though the air was balmy, she found herself shivering. 'How did you know I'd be in the park?'

'I waited in the mews until I saw you leave the gallery, then I followed you.'

'*Why* did you follow me?' she demanded.

White teeth gleamed in a wolfish smile. 'I thought it was high time we had a talk.'

'As far as I'm concerned, there's nothing to say.' She jumped to her feet and took an unsteady step.

'Don't rush off.' He reached out, and his fingers closed lightly but inexorably around her wrist.

'Let me go,' she said jerkily. 'I don't want to talk to you.'

He drew her back to the bench and, careful not to hurt her, applied just enough downward pressure to make it expedient to sit.

When she sank down onto the wooden slats, he smiled a little. 'Well, if you really don't want to talk, I can think of more exciting things to do.' His eyes were fixed on her mouth.

Her voice shrill with panic, she cried, 'No!'

'Shame,' he drawled. 'Though it seems an age since I last kissed you, I can still remember how passionately you used to respond. You'd make little mewing noises in your throat, your nipples would grow firm and—'

She went hot all over and, seeing nothing else for it,

threw in the towel. 'What did you want to talk to me about?'

'I want to know why you ran away. Why you left me without a word...'

Normally, he had a warm, attractive voice, a voice that had always charmed her. Now the underlying ice in it sent a chill right down her spine.

'Why you didn't at least tell me what was wrong.'

Feeling a deep and bitter anger, she wrenched her wrist free and rounded on him, eyes flashing. 'How can you pretend to be so innocent? Pretend not to know "what was wrong"?'

He sighed. 'Perhaps you could save the histrionics and just tell me?'

Unwilling to reveal the extent of her hurt, her desolation, she choked back the angry accusations, and said wearily, 'It's over two years ago. I can't see that it matters now...'

Of course it mattered. It would always matter.

'We're different people. The girl I was then no longer exists.'

'You've certainly altered,' he admitted, studying her oval face: the pure bone structure, the long-lashed greeny-grey eyes beneath winged brows, the short straight nose, and lovely passionate mouth.

'Then, you were young and innocent, radiantly pretty, almost incandescent...'

If she had been, love had made her that way. Happiness was a great beautifier.

'Now you've—' His voice suddenly impeded, he stopped speaking abruptly.

But she knew well enough what he'd been about to say. Each morning her mirror showed her a woman who had come up against life and lost. A woman whose sparkle had gone, and who was vulnerable, with sad eyes and, despite all her efforts to smile, a mouth that drooped a little at the corners.

She swallowed hard. 'I'm surprised you recognised me from just that brief glimpse.'

'I almost didn't. That severe hairstyle and those glasses change your appearance significantly, and the "Miss Ashley" had me wondering. If I hadn't been expecting to see you—'

'So you *knew* I was there?' she broke in sharply.

'Oh, yes, I knew. I've known for some time. Did you really think I wouldn't find you?'

Rather than answer, she chose to ask a question of her own, 'What made you come into the gallery?'

'I decided to check things out on a personal level.'

'You told Charles that you wanted to buy *Wednesday's Child*.'

'So I do.'

'Why?'

'Surely you can guess. Will he be able to get it for me, do you think?'

'I've no idea.'

'But not if you can help it?'

When she made no comment, he added with a smile, 'Though I guess I won't need *Wednesday's Child* when I've got the real thing.'

Afraid to ask what he meant by that, she remained silent, looking anywhere but at him.

'From Raynor's manner,' Ryan went on, 'I rather gathered you'd kept quiet about our…shall we say…relationship?'

'It's not something I like to talk about.'

He pulled a face at her tone. 'So how much did you have to tell him in the end, to get him to see me in your place?'

'I just said you were someone I'd once known and didn't want to meet again.'

'How very understated and cold-blooded.'

'It happens to be the truth.'

She saw his face grow taut with anger, before a shutter came down leaving an expressionless mask.

'I would have said I was rather more than someone you'd once known even if you're using the word known in its biblical sense.'

She moved restlessly, desperate to get away, but knowing she stood no chance until he was willing to let her go.

'That's all in the past,' she said tightly. 'Over and done with.'

'Hardly.'

'It's over and done with as far as I'm concerned.'

He shook his head. 'That's where you're wrong. I want you back.'

'What?'

Though he had sworn, 'I'll never let you go,' the fact that she *had* gone, had run away and left him, should surely have hurt his pride to the point where he wouldn't want her back under any circumstances?

'I want you back,' he repeated flatly.

Stammering in her agitation, she cried, 'I'll never c-come back to you.'

'Never is a long time,' he said lightly.

'I mean it, Ryan. There's nothing you can do or say that will make me change my mind.'

'I don't think you should bet on it.' His little crooked smile made her blood run cold.

'Please, Ryan…' She found she was begging. 'I've made a new life for myself and I just want to be left to enjoy it.'

'You once told me you disliked being on your own.'

'I'm not on my own.' The words were defiant, meant to make an impression.

'Let's get this straight, we *are* talking about merely sharing accommodation?'

'*I* wasn't,' she said boldly. If he believed she was seriously involved with someone else he might leave her alone; she wouldn't let herself be hurt again.

He froze into stillness, before asking quietly, 'So, who are you sleeping with?'

'It's none of your business.'

'I'm making it my business.' Those indigo eyes pinning her, he repeated, 'Who?'

'Charles.'

Ryan laughed incredulously. 'That middle-aged wimp?'

'Don't you dare call Charles a wimp. He's nothing of the kind. He's sweet and sensitive, and I owe him a big debt of gratitude. He gave me a job and a home when I was desperate.'

'I'm quite aware that you share his house—my detective has followed the pair of you home often enough—but knowing you as I do, I hesitate to believe that *gratitude* is enough to get you into his bed.'

'It isn't just gratitude. I happen to love him. Passionately,' she added for good measure.

Ryan's mocking smile told her he didn't believe a word of it. 'So, when did you two become lovers?'

'Ages ago.'

'Then, how is it you have separate bedrooms?'

'What makes you think we have separate bedrooms?'

'I don't think. I *know*.'

'How could you possibly know a thing like that?' she scoffed.

'With a bit of encouragement, the domestic help can be an excellent source of information. Mrs Crabtree, in particular, enjoys a good gossip.'

Virginia's heart sank. Mrs Crabtree, a cheerful, garrulous woman, came in several times a week to clean and tidy.

Seeing nothing else for it, she admitted, 'All right, so we have separate bedrooms. Charles is conventional enough to want to keep up appearances.'

'That's not surprising. He's old enough to be your father.'

'He's nothing of the kind.'

'Rubbish! He must be forty-five if he's a day.'

'Charles is forty-three. In any case, age has nothing to do with it. He's a wonderful lover.'

Even as she spoke she felt a stab of conscience. It was hardly fair to Charles to *use* him in this way; perhaps she should just tell Ryan the truth... But she'd gone much too far to back down now.

Recklessly, she added, 'And he's not hidebound enough to believe that lovemaking should only take place in bed.'

A dangerous light in his eyes, Ryan said, 'I hope for everyone's sake that you're lying.'

'Did you seriously expect me to be living like a nun?'

'You were when I met you.'

'In those days I was abysmally naive and innocent. But you taught me a lot, and it's much more difficult to give up a *known* pleasure.'

Watching him weighing up her words, wondering...she struck at his ego, 'Or did you think you were the only man who could turn me on?'

'I certainly didn't think Raynor was your type.'

'That just shows how wrong you can be. Charles and I are very good together. He wants to marry me.'

A dark flush appeared along Ryan's high cheekbones. 'Over my dead body. I've no intention of letting anyone else have you.'

Rattled, she found herself catching at straws. 'But you said yourself how much I've changed. I'm not even pretty any longer.'

'No, you're not merely *pretty*. Now you have the kind of poignant beauty that's haunting.'

She half shook her head. 'Even it that were true, the world's full of beautiful women.'

One in particular.

'In the past I've had my share of beautiful women. But

I find that, after you, none of them will do. It's you I want in my bed and in my life.'

'I don't understand *why*,' she cried desperately.

His voice cold as steel, he said, 'For one thing, there's a score to settle. You owe me.'

CHAPTER TWO

WHITE to the lips, she whispered, 'A score to settle?'

'Why should that surprise you? You must have known that leaving me as you did would make me look a complete and utter fool?'

She couldn't even deny it. Part of her had *wanted* to pay him back. *Wanted* to wound him as much as he'd wounded her. *Wanted* to destroy his world, as he'd destroyed hers.

Afraid that he might read it in her eyes, she looked away, watching a small boy in a blue T-shirt and red shorts run towards the lake. He was clutching a shining new toy yacht, obviously a birthday present, and a stick.

As he knelt on the low parapet to launch the vessel into the water, his mother, who was wheeling a baby in a pushchair, called, 'Be careful, Thomas. Don't fall in. The water's deep.'

When—his will was proving stronger than hers—Virginia's eyes were drawn irresistibly back to Ryan's, he pursued. 'Apart from that, when you just disappeared and I had no idea where you were or what had happened to you, I nearly went out of my mind with worry. Since then I've spent two-and-a-half years and a small fortune looking for you.

'Now I've found you, I want you in my bed. I want to make love to you until you're begging for mercy and I'm sated. Then I want to start all over again. Does the thought of being made love to until you're begging for mercy turn you on?'

Heat running through her, she said thickly, 'No! I can't bear the thought of you touching me.'

His handsome eyes gleamed. 'Knowing that will give me great satisfaction, and add immeasurably to my pleasure—'

A simultaneous yelp of fright, a splash, and a high-pitched scream cut through his words.

Ryan was on his feet in an instant and running towards the lake as the woman with the pushchair continued to scream hysterically.

He said something short and sharp to her that stopped the screaming, and a second later he had cleared the parapet and had plunged into the water.

Rooted to the spot, Virginia watched him haul the small dripping figure from the lake and set him on his shoulders. Judging by the roars of fright the child was letting forth, he was mercifully uninjured.

The water was somewhere in the region of three-and-a-half feet deep, and came past Ryan's waist, as he waded a few steps to rescue the capsized yacht.

Letting go of the pushchair, the woman, now sobbing loudly with relief, hovered, arms outstretched ready to embrace her son.

Belatedly, Virginia's brain kicked into action, and realising that no real harm had been done, she grabbed her bag and leaving Ryan to cope, bolted.

Hurrying as fast as she could to the nearest of the park's side entrances, she made her way between the ornate metal bollards and out onto busy Kenelm Road.

A black cab was cruising past and, hailing it, she pulled open the door and jumped in, breathing hard, her heart racing.

'Where to, lady?'

'Sixteen Usher Street.'

Sinking back, drenched in perspiration, she glanced in the direction of the park. There was no sign of pursuit and, starting to tremble in every limb, she sent up a silent prayer of thanks. She'd escaped.

But for how long?

Ryan knew all about her. Where she worked, where she lived, her movements... He had said he wanted her back, and he wasn't a man to give up.

Just seeing him again had shaken her to the core, but the knowledge that he wanted her back had been even more traumatic.

It had been so entirely *unexpected*. Never once had she considered the possibility that he might want her back again.

It was unthinkable. The very idea made her blood turn to ice in her veins. All he wanted was revenge. He didn't even love her.

If he'd loved her, it might have been different...

But if he'd loved her she would never have left him in the first place...

Her hectic thoughts were interrupted by the taxi turning into Usher Street and coming to a halt in front of number sixteen.

It was a quiet street of cream-stuccoed town houses with basements guarded by black wrought-iron railings, and steps leading up to elegant front doors with fluted fanlights.

Charles had inherited the house from his parents, some five years previously. A confirmed bachelor, at least until Virginia had come along, he'd talked about moving somewhere smaller, easier to manage. But in truth he was comfortable there, and it was reasonably close to the gallery.

Recalling agitatedly what Ryan had said about his detective following her, Virginia suddenly felt uncomfortable.

She scrambled out of the taxi and, having reached through the window to pay the driver, ran up the steps to let herself in.

Feeling invisible eyes boring into her back, her palms grew clammy, and pointing the truth of the saying, more haste less speed, it took several attempts to turn the key in the lock.

Her heart throwing itself against her ribs, she dropped

the key into her purse, slammed the door behind her, and hurried through the hall and into a large attractively furnished living-room with long windows.

Dropping her bag on the couch she crossed the room and peered cautiously from behind the curtains, half expecting to see a strange man opposite, lurking behind a newspaper.

Apart from a woman walking past whom she recognised as a neighbour, the sunny, tree-lined street was deserted.

With a feeling of anticlimax, Virginia told herself satirically that she was either getting paranoid, or had been watching too many detective series on the television.

But her attempt to josh herself out of it failed dismally. The threat to her new-found security was chillingly real and couldn't be laughed away.

Becoming aware that her head was now throbbing fiercely, she went into the kitchen to make herself a cup of tea and swallow a couple of painkillers.

Then, uncomfortably hot and sticky, she decided to have a shower and wash her hair. Physically, at least, that should make her feel better.

She stripped off her clothes and, removing the pins from her hair, shook it loose before stepping beneath the jet of warm water.

As she reached for the shampoo, she found herself wondering about Ryan. He must have been saturated...

Had he walked back to his hotel? Or braved it out and hailed a taxi? Was he at this precise minute also taking a shower?

In the old days, alone in his Fifth Avenue penthouse, they had enjoyed showering together...

While the scented steam rose and billowed, her own hands stilled as she recalled how *his* hands had roamed over her slick body, caressing her slender curves, cupping her buttocks, stroking her thighs, finding the nest of wet brown curls, while his tongue licked drops of water from her nipples...

Shuddering at the erotic memory she turned off the water and, winding a towel turban-fashion around her head, began to dry herself with unnecessary vigour, rubbing the pale gold skin until it glowed pink.

Having decided not to bother and get dressed again, she found the Christmas present Charles had given her, a chenille robe-cum-housecoat in moss green and, pulling it on, belted it.

Her feet bare, her naturally curly hair still damp and loose around her shoulders, she was descending the stairs when the phone in the hall began to chirrup.

Reaching out a hand she was about to pick up the receiver when it occurred to her that it might be Ryan, and she hesitated.

Who else was likely to be calling? Who else would know she was home before her usual time?

It kept chirruping, and its sheer persistence tearing at her nerves, she snatched it up.

'Virginia?' It was Charles. His well-modulated voice sounded a shade anxious.

'Yes,' she said hurriedly. 'Yes, I'm here.'

'Is anything wrong?'

She took a deep breath. 'No, of course not.'

'You didn't seem to be answering.'

'I've just got out of the shower.' It wasn't exactly a lie.

'Oh, I see.'

'Is there a problem?' she asked.

'No. Not at all... I was just ringing to make sure you were all right.'

'Yes, I'm fine.'

'Certain?' With his usual sensitivity he had picked up her jumpiness.

Resisting the impulse to tell him about Ryan and beg him to come home, she said with what cheerfulness she could muster, 'Absolutely. Any idea what time you'll be back?'

'I should be home somewhere around eight-thirty. Don't forget to save me some prawn crackers.'

'I won't,' she promised. 'Bye for now.'

As she replaced the handset, the grandmother clock whirred and began to chime six-thirty.

Might as well ring for her takeaway now, she decided. It usually took between thirty and forty minutes for an order to be delivered, and she'd only had part of a roll for lunch, the remainder having been fed to a family of sparrows who, nesting in the eaves above her office window, had learnt to line up along the sill, bright-eyed and expectant.

Not that she was hungry.

But something to eat might help to get rid of the hollow, stomach-churning feeling that had persisted since Ryan had said, 'Guess who?' in the park.

The number of the restaurant was written in Charles's neat numerals in the book by the phone, but it was Ryan's face that swam before her eyes as she tapped in the digits.

'The Jade Garden. Good evening...' a singsong voice responded.

Her mind still obsessed by Ryan, Virginia, who was usually clear and precise, made a mess of her order and was forced to stumble through it a second time.

Returning to the living-room, she prowled about plumping cushions and tidying magazines, far too restless to sit still.

What would Ryan do next? she wondered anxiously. There was no doubt in her mind that he wouldn't let matters rest. He wanted her, and his sense of purpose was terrifying...

Though she had lied through her teeth about her relationship with Charles, it hadn't had the desired effect. Ryan either hadn't believed her, or hadn't wanted to.

Either way, her assertions had failed to provide the anchor, the safeguard, she had been so desperate to put in place.

But even if he *had* believed her, would that have stopped him? Remembering the look on his face when he'd said, 'I've no intention of letting anyone else have you', she felt her skin goose-flesh.

Just seeing him again, feeling the force of his will, had made her doubt her ability to hold out against him if he kept up the seige.

No! she mustn't think like that. If necessary she would tell Charles the whole truth, and beg for his forgiveness and support.

He was far from being the wimp that Ryan had so contemptuously called him. In fact, in a different and less obvious way he was as strong as Ryan, with a quiet determination and a tensile strength.

But how could she ask Charles for help, ask him to pretend to be her lover, when she had denied him that privilege by refusing his proposal of marriage?

All at once she was filled with a burning shame that she'd even considered involving him any further. Somehow she *must* manage without his help.

There was one thing in her favour. Usually a brilliant strategist, this time Ryan had made a bad mistake. He had admitted that he was out to make her pay for leaving him, and forewarned was forearmed.

Though his attraction was as powerful as ever, knowing his intentions would enable her to hold out against him, to freeze him off...

The peal of the doorbell interrupted her thoughts.

Her takeaway had come a lot quicker than usual. But of course it was still quite early. They wouldn't yet have had a build-up of customers...

She fumbled in her bag and purse in hand, went to open the door.

Taken completely by surprise, her reactions were a trifle slow and, before she could slam the door in his face, Ryan had slipped inside.

Over six feet tall and broad-shouldered, he seemed to fill the small hall.

Closing the door behind him he stood leaning with his back to the panels. Wearing stone-coloured trousers and a two-tone, smart-casual jacket, he looked tanned and fit and dangerous.

'Get out!' she cried in a panic. 'You have no right to force your way in here.'

'I didn't exactly *force* my way in,' he objected, adding coolly, 'Though I might well have done had it proved necessary.'

Surveying the robe, her shiny face and the wealth of ash-brown hair curling loosely around her shoulders, he remarked, 'You look about ready for bed. But of course Raynor doesn't take you to bed, does he? He has more...shall we say...inventive ideas.'

When, her soft lips tightening, she said nothing, he goaded, 'Tell me, Virginia, where does he usually make love to you? In the kitchen? Lying in front of the fire? On the stairs?'

'Stop it!' she cried.

'After what you told me earlier, you can't blame me for being curious.'

Wishing fervently that she'd kept her mouth shut, she said, 'I want you to go. Now! Before Charles gets home. He won't be long.'

Ryan shook his head. 'It's no use, Virginia, my sweet, I know perfectly well that he won't be in until much later...'

How did he know?

'And, even if that wasn't the case, do you seriously think the prospect of Raynor coming home would scare me into leaving?'

No, she didn't. Lifting her chin, she threatened, 'I could always call the police.'

'You *could*,' he agreed, 'but somehow I don't think you will. After all, the police have a lot more to concern themselves about than what they would undoubtedly class as a trivial domestic problem.'

In past skirmishes he had proved to be quicker witted than she was, and in any battle of words he almost invariably won. But she couldn't allow him to win this time.

'It isn't "a trivial domestic problem,"' she said through gritted teeth. 'It's an illegal entry into someone else's home.'

'How can it be an "illegal entry" when you opened the door to me yourself?'

'I thought it was my takeaway.'

Eyeing the purse she was still holding, he said, 'I see. Well, if you have a meal ordered, perhaps you'll invite me to stay and share it?'

Her agitation increasing, she cried, 'No, I don't want you to stay. I don't know why you came in the first place.'

'For one thing, we hadn't finished our conversation—'

'There's nothing further to say. I'll never come back to you, so you're just wasting your time.'

As though she hadn't interrupted, he went on, his voice quietly lethal, 'And for another, I'm not prepared to let you keep running out on me.'

For the first time she realised he was furiously angry, and she quailed inwardly.

He stepped towards her, dwarfing her five feet seven inches, and with a hand beneath her chin, he forced it up. His eyes were focussed on her mouth, his dark face sharp and intent.

Guessing his intention, she begged, 'No! Oh, please, Ryan, don't...'

But his hand slid round to her nape, tangling in her silky hair, and his mouth swooped down on hers, taking possession, stifling any further protests.

The purse she had been clutching like a lifeline thudded to the floor and, despite all her efforts to hold aloof, the blood began to pound in her ears and the world tilted on its axis.

Head spinning, she was engulfed, gathered up and swept away on a tide of conflicting emotions, while every nerve ending in her body zinged into life.

At first his kiss was hard, punitive, a way of venting his anger, the arm clamping her to him like an iron band.

But when, scarcely able to stand, she made no attempt to break free, his arm loosened its hold slightly and, instead of being a punishment, his kiss became passionate, his skilful tongue sending shivers of excitement and pleasure running through her.

Leaving her nape, his hand slid inside the lapels of her robe, following her collarbone, moving down to find and fondle the soft curve of her breast.

He seemed to be deliberately avoiding the tip and, desperate for his touch, her whole being was poised in an agony of waiting.

When, finally, his experienced fingers began to lightly tease the sensitive nipple, causing sensations so exquisite they were almost pain, her stomach clenched and a core of liquid heat began to form in her abdomen.

Now he was making her feel all that he wanted her to feel, and he took her little gasps and whimpers into his mouth like the conqueror he was.

Lost and mindless, she was hardly aware when his free hand undid the belt and eased the robe from her shoulders, allowing it to fall at her feet.

His mouth had moved away from hers to rove over the smooth flesh he had exposed, when, shockingly, the doorbell rang.

Ryan's recovery was light years ahead of Virginia's. Stooping, he gathered up the robe and, wrapping it around her, gently hustled her across the hall and into the kitchen.

Pulling on the robe with shaking hands, she belted it

tightly and, sinking down in the nearest chair, groaned aloud.

So much for holding out against him.

Oh, dear Lord, what had she been thinking of? If it hadn't been for the interruption, Ryan could have taken her right there on the hall carpet and she would have allowed it.

No, more than allowed it, *welcomed* it.

Oh, you fool! she berated herself. She had planned to freeze him off, to make it clear that she was no longer under his spell.

Instead her abject surrender must have boosted his confidence, made him even more certain that he could win...

Only he mustn't. Much as she wanted him—and she did still want him, maybe she always would—she mustn't let him win.

Through her tumult of mind she was aware of the front door opening and Ryan's voice saying, 'Thanks. How much do I owe you?'

By the time he came through to the kitchen carrying a brightly coloured cardboard box with a handle, she had gathered the remnants of her dignity around her like a tattered cloak.

Standing up, she faced him squarely. 'I want you to leave, now, this minute.'

Unpacking the various foil containers onto the pine table, he said mildly, 'I like Chinese food and, as you appear to have ordered enough for two, it would be a shame to waste it.'

Looking dazedly at the number of containers, she realised that her repeat of the order had caused confusion and had resulted in them delivering far too much food.

Watching her face, he asked ironically, 'Was it a Freudian slip? Did you subconsciously want or expect me to be here?'

'No, I certainly didn't. If I wanted anyone here, it would be Charles.'

She could tell by the way Ryan's mouth tightened that her answer had annoyed him, but all he said was, 'Do you have any bowls and chopsticks?'

'In the cupboard,' she answered shortly. He might insist on staying, but that didn't mean she was prepared to make him welcome.

Slipping out of his jacket, he hung it over the back of a chair before opening the cupboard door.

Along with the bowls was a small electric hotplate. Infuriatingly at home, he took it out and, having plugged it in, arranged the foil containers on it.

Loosening the lids, he suggested, 'Why don't you sit down and tell me what you'd like to start with?'

Still standing, she said curtly, 'I don't want anything to eat. I've lost my appetite.'

He raised dark level brows. 'That's a pity. Still if you're *quite* sure you don't want to eat, we could always start a precedent.'

Alarmed by the silky menace in his tone, the glint in his eye, she demanded, 'What do you mean, start a precedent?'

'Don't you think it would be a nice change to be carried upstairs and made love to *in bed*?'

All the fight going out of her, she sat down abruptly.

White teeth gleamed as he laughed. 'No? Oh, well...' Taking a seat opposite, he queried, 'So what's it to be? The sesame prawn toast looks good.' Leaning towards her, he offered her a piece.

His dark silk shirt was open at the neck, exposing the strong column of his throat. Remembering how she had sometimes buried her face against it when he'd made love to her, her mouth went dry.

Lifting her eyes, she met his ironic gaze, and felt the colour flood into her cheeks.

'You look warm,' he observed innocently. 'Do you have any nice cool wine?'

Somehow she managed to say, 'There's a bottle open in the fridge.'

He found a couple of glasses and filled them with Chablis. Then, having helped them both to chicken and cashew nuts, he picked up his bamboo chopsticks and, sorting out one of the fat, gleaming cashews, reached across the table.

Without conscious volition, her mouth opened and he popped it in.

His action was like a blow to the solar plexus, winding her and making her heart thump erratically.

Eating their first meal together in New York's Chinatown, she had mentioned that she only ordered that particular dish because she adored cashew nuts.

Loverlike, he had fed her the nuts from his own bowl. After that it had become a kind of tender ritual.

Except, of course, that it had only been play-acting. He might have wanted her, he undoubtedly had, but he had never loved her, had never felt any real tenderness for her. He had just wanted to use her.

But she had refused to be used, though it had broken her heart to leave him...

As though following her train of thought, Ryan said abruptly, 'You still haven't told me why you ran the way you did.'

'You ought to know.'

'If it was what I can only presume it was—'

'Did you think I wouldn't mind?' she burst out. 'Think I'd play along, let you use me and say nothing?'

He frowned. 'I haven't the faintest idea what you're talking about. You'd better explain.'

Infuriated by his denial, she jumped to her feet. 'I've no intention of *explaining* anything. I want you to go, and if you won't go, then I will!'

As she turned away, he said quietly, 'Sit down and finish your meal.'

Their glances met and clashed.

She wanted to disobey his order, to walk away, but she couldn't leave, and she found herself subsiding into her chair.

After a moment, he asked softly, 'Why didn't you at least let me know you were safe?'

'Why do you suppose?'

'You didn't think I might worry about you?'

'I tried not to think of you at all.'

'What about the rest of the family?'

When she said nothing, he went on, 'They were all very upset and concerned that you'd gone without a word. Beth in particular…'

'I'm sorry about that. I liked your stepmother.' It was the truth. In fact, with one exception, she'd liked the whole family.

'She had another heart attack,' he added flatly.

Virginia caught her breath.

Seeing the apprehension on her face, Ryan said quickly, 'A fairly mild one, thank the Lord.'

'Then, she's all right?'

'She made a good recovery. Which is just as well.'

'You mean if she hadn't, you would have held me responsible?'

'I *do* hold you responsible.'

Virginia flinched at the bitter irony. It had been mainly to safeguard his stepmother's fragile state of health that she had chosen to run as she did.

'Do Janice and Steven?'

'What do you think?'

Her heart sank. Still, it was better that they should blame her, a comparative stranger, rather than know something that would almost certainly tear their close-knit family apart.

One half of her still wondered incredulously how Ryan had been able to do what he did. But perhaps he'd found it impossible to help himself? Love could be a powerful, overriding force...

As could the need for revenge.

Though more sinned against than sinning, she had wrecked all his carefully laid plans and, in his own eyes at least, had made him look a fool.

Not something a man like him would easily forgive.

She shivered.

'You're surely not cold?' Ryan asked.

'No.'

'Ashamed?'

'Why should *I* be ashamed?'

'I can think of several good reasons. First and foremost that you treated a woman, who had taken you to her heart, in such a callous fashion...'

Perhaps, in retrospect, she *should* have left a note, made up some excuse for going... But, shocked and stunned, feeling mortally wounded, she hadn't known what to say.

'I'm sorry if it seemed that way. I never meant to hurt her...'

A shrill bleating cut through her words.

'Excuse me.' Reaching into his jacket pocket he produced a mobile phone. 'Falconer... It has? Good... Yes... Yes... Be with you shortly.'

Dropping the phone back in his pocket, he rose to his feet and pulled on his jacket. 'I'm sorry I have to leave quite so soon.'

'I'm afraid I can't say the same,' she informed him trenchantly.

Paying her back for her show of spirit, he came round the table and with studied insolence slipped his hand inside the lapels of her robe and cupped her breast.

Knowing that he was waiting for her to jump up and

protest, summoning every last ounce of will-power, she sat still and silent.

Smiling a little, he bent his dark head and his mouth brushed hers. 'When you're in bed on your own tonight, dream that I'm making love to you.'

'Not if I can help it,' she spat at him.

'If you're frustrated enough, you might find it impossible not to.'

'I'm *not* frustrated.'

Smiling, he rubbed his thumb over the nipple until it firmed. 'You were always very responsive.'

Unable to stand any more, she jerked away and, dragging the lapels together, jumped to her feet. 'Aren't you forgetting something? Or should I say, someone?'

His blue-violet eyes narrowed.

'Charles might not be a young man by your standards, but he's fit and in his prime. If I am frustrated I won't need to stay that way.'

She saw a white line appear round Ryan's mouth and, fiercely glad that he was furious, laughed in his face.

With a sound almost like a growl, he took her upper arms, his fingers biting into the soft flesh, and warned softly, 'Don't even *think* about it. From now on I intend to be the only man in your life, so if Raynor does get any bright ideas about making love to you, it will pay you to say no, and mean it.'

Dragging her right up against him, he kissed her once more. This time his kiss was hard and unsparing, rocking her to her very foundations. Then suddenly she was free.

'Be seeing you,' he said mockingly.

A moment later she heard the front door open and close.

Badly shaken, she went through to the hall on unsteady legs. Ryan was gone, but she noted abstractedly that her purse had been picked up and placed neatly on the telephone table.

Trembling now as reaction set in, she sank down on the

bottom step of the stairs and stared blindly into space while her thoughts whirled.

Oh, dear Lord, what was she to do? Ryan's unwelcome visit had proved at least two terrifying things: that he was in deadly earnest; and that her chances of resisting him were practically nil.

It had been that way from the start. She had looked at him and had loved him, heart and soul.

Recognising at some deep, subconscious level that he was the one she had been waiting all her life for, she had given herself to him with a joyous certainty, and the hope of a happy ever after.

But that happy ever after had been short-lived. A bare two months from its rapturous start to its bitter ending...

And now, unless she could find some way of keeping Ryan at bay, the torture would start all over again.

She would still be there, and even if his feelings for the other woman—love or obsession, call it what one will—had died, the situation would still be quite intolerable.

No matter what he said about wanting only *her*, Virginia knew that she would never again be able to believe nor trust him. And he must know that... It might even be part of his revenge to have her on the rack of jealousy and torment...

No, no, she couldn't, *wouldn't* go back to him.

But, even as she tried to make herself believe it, she knew she was like a moth that, unable to help itself, was drawn irresistibly and fatally towards a candle flame.

CHAPTER THREE

GRITTING her teeth, she tried to reject that frightening image. Somehow she must help herself. Find a way out of still loving Ryan.

If only she had loved Charles enough to marry him... But it wasn't so much a case of not loving Charles, as of still loving Ryan.

Though how could she go on loving a man who hated her? Who only wanted to hurt her? It was utter madness. That kind of self-destructive love could end up wrecking her whole life.

If she allowed it to.

But even if she was strong enough to hold out against him, all she had to look forward to was an empty future.

As far as she was concerned, love and sex went hand in hand. She wasn't one for casual sex nor for affairs, but she was a young woman still with natural needs.

True those needs had been smothered and suppressed for over two-and-a-half years, but how quickly they had flared into life as soon as Ryan had kissed her.

If she didn't want to live like a nun, marrying Charles, a man she was fond of and respected, was the obvious answer. She would be safe then, her future more hopeful, with the prospect of children and a happy, family life.

As for her reservations about it not being fair to him, well, she had told him honestly how she felt, and he'd said he was willing to try...

So why not? It might be no grande passion, at least on her side, but if she could make him happy...

The clock chiming eight roused her. With a bit of luck, Charles would be home in about half an hour.

Getting to her feet, she went back to the kitchen and, making a determined effort to think about the brighter future she had envisaged, rather than the unhappy past, began to wash up and clear away the debris of the meal.

She had only just finished and plugged in the kettle when she heard the sound of Charles's key in the lock.

Hurrying through to the hall, she smiled at him. 'You're back nice and early.'

Hearing the relief in her voice, he was glad that he'd hurried straight home rather than going on to a pub, as his companion had suggested when their business was over.

'How did your appointment go?'

'Very well.'

'That's good.'

She sounded distracted, he thought, as though her mind was on other things.

Studying her pale, drawn face, he asked gently, 'Headache still bothering you?'

'No, not really. I took some tablets when I first got home. By the way, the kettle's on if you'd like some coffee?'

'Love some.'

Wearing the robe he had bought her, and with her curly hair tumbling around her shoulders, he thought she had never looked so lovely. Nor so fraught. Something had happened to seriously upset her.

Wondering if she wanted to talk about it, or if she would prefer to be alone, he asked carefully, 'Were you thinking of having an early night?'

Shaking her head, she explained, 'I didn't bother getting dressed again after my shower.'

'Then if you're not off to bed, why don't you have some coffee with me?'

'Yes, I'd like to. There's something I want to tell you.'

He hung up the jacket of his suit, and was starting to follow her into the kitchen when she said hastily, 'I'll bring it through to the living-room.'

The kitchen was still uncomfortably full of Ryan's presence.

When she had filled the cafetière and had put the coffee things on the tray, she carried it in and set it down on the low table.

The west-facing room, always pleasant in the evening, was full of low sun, which threw a distorted pattern of oblong window panes and leafy branches onto the magnolia walls.

She poured the coffee, stirred sugar and cream into his, and handed it to him.

'Thank you. I don't know what I've done to deserve being waited on,' he remarked humorously.

Too tense to sit still, she left her own cup untouched and, wandering over to the window, stood looking out while the silence lengthened.

Now the moment had arrived, she had no idea how to broach the subject.

Watching her and guessing her difficulty, he said, 'What was it you wanted to tell me?'

Still she hesitated. Suppose he'd had second thoughts about his proposal? Decided it had been a mistake?

Well there was only one way to find out. Turning, she took the bull by the horns. 'When you asked me to marry you, you said if I ever changed my mind the offer would still be open…'

Thrown, because it was the last thing he'd expected her to say, it was a second or two before he assured her, 'It is.'

As she let out the breath she'd been unconsciously holding, his blue eyes filled with a dawning hope, he asked urgently, '*Have* you changed your mind?'

'Yes. I will marry you, if you still want me to.'

'Darling!' He was on his feet and gathering her close, eager as a boy. 'Believe me, I've never wanted anything more.'

He held her firmly, with no sign of diffidence, and his kiss was pleasant, almost exciting.

After a while he stopped kissing her to ask, 'What made you change your mind?'

'Well, I...I got to thinking... I'd like a husband and a home and a family... You do want children?' she added a shade anxiously.

'I'd never actually thought about it,' he answered honestly. 'But if that's what it takes to make you happy... How many were you thinking of?' He sounded like a man on a high, a man who could hardly believe his luck.

'At least two, possibly three or four.'

'Why stop at four?' he teased.

'Charles... You are quite certain this is what you want? A wife and family, I mean?'

'Quite certain. Forty-three isn't too old.'

'No, of course it isn't.'

'But I'm not getting any younger, so how soon will you marry me?'

'As soon as you want.'

'What kind of wedding would you like?'

'A quiet one.'

'You don't want a white dress with all the trimmings?'

Knowing she must tell him the truth, she said flatly, 'White is the sign of virginity.'

'And you're not a virgin?'

'No. I'm sorry if that bothers you.'

'My darling, I'm not Victorian enough to support the old double standard. Though I've been fairly circumspect in my dealings with women, I certainly haven't lived like a monk, and I wouldn't expect a woman of twenty-four never to have had lovers—'

'Not lovers in the plural,' she said quietly.

'One special one?'

'Yes.'

His heart sank. Several lovers that didn't really matter

was one thing… One special lover that, judging by her face, mattered a great deal was another.

Remembering Virginia's reaction to the dark, powerful-looking man who had come into the gallery that afternoon, he said, 'It was Ryan Falconer, wasn't it?'

Moistening her dry lips, she nodded.

He drew her over to the settee and when she sank down on the soft cushions, took a seat by her side. 'I think you'd better tell me about him.'

The last person she wanted to talk about just at that minute was Ryan, and half hoping for a reprieve, she stammered, 'I—I don't know where to start.'

'Start at the beginning,' Charles suggested quietly.

Seeing no help for it, she gathered herself, and began. 'It's getting on for three years since we first met. I'd left art school and was working in the Trantor Gallery, when late one morning a man came in…'

While she told him the bare bones of it, memory fleshed out the details and she relived the past as though it was the present…

The gallery was quiet, as it usually was towards noon, just an elderly couple browsing, and a small group of men in business suits discussing the relative merits of two abstract paintings.

Sitting behind the polished-wood reception desk, Virginia was checking the contents of a catalogue when the smoked glass door opened and a man came in and strolled across.

Tall and well-built, with thick dark hair that tried to curl a little, he was dressed in the latest smart-casual De Quincy jacket and handmade shoes.

As he got closer she could see he was somewhere in his early thirties, with a tough, masculine face, strong features and a beautiful mouth.

He was one of the most attractive men she had ever seen.

No, more than just attractive, he was what Marsha would have termed drop-dead gorgeous.

'Miss Adams?' The most incredible blue-violet eyes, with faint laughter lines at the corners, smiled into hers.

Virginia found it quite impossible not to stare into those eyes and, instantly captivated, her mouth went dry, and her heartbeat quickened.

Wits scattered, she stammered, 'Y-yes.'

'My name's Ryan Falconer. I'm acquainted with your parents.'

'They live in New York,' she said stupidly.

White teeth flashed in a smile. 'Yes, I know, I had lunch with them a couple of days ago, and they told me where to find you...'

He had a nice voice, warm and slightly husky, with a not-too-pronounced American accent.

'There's something I'd like to discuss with you, so perhaps you'll allow me to take you out to lunch?'

Excitement and disappointment mingling, she said, 'I usually just have a yoghurt...'

'Well, I had thought of something a little more substantial,' he mocked gently, 'but if a yoghurt is all you can eat...'

Flustered because he was laughing at her, she explained, 'It's not that. You see at the moment there's no one to take my place. Marsha's ill, so I'm only able to have about a ten-minute break.'

He glanced around the gallery. 'You surely can't be here all alone?'

'Oh, no. Both Mr and Mrs Trantor are in the office.'

'Which is?'

'The door on the left.'

'I'll have a word.'

Quickly, she said, 'I'd rather you didn't.'

He cocked a dark level brow at her. 'You really don't want to have lunch with me?'

'It's not that. But I don't think they'd agree to my going out—'

'Oh, I think they might.'

Bearing in mind the exorbitant rent she had to pay for her small and somewhat dingy two-roomed flat, she begged, 'Please, Mr Falconer, I've just taken over a furnished flat, so I can't afford to lose my job—'

'Ryan, please. And there'll be no question of you losing your job.'

Before she could protest any further, he advanced purposefully on the door, tapped and walked in, rather as if he owned the place.

Holding her breath, she stared after him helplessly.

He returned quite quickly, with Mrs Trantor leading the way. To Virginia's amazement the woman usually referred to as the Dragon was smiling, even fluttering a little.

'No, of course I don't mind, Mr Falconer. I'll be happy to take care of reception myself. Off you go, Miss Adams.'

Stumbling over her thanks, Virginia hurried to fetch her jacket and bag, pausing only to pull a comb through her silky curls. A few seconds later she was being escorted outside.

It was a cold, crisp day in early October, with sunshine lighting the autumn colours, and drifts of brown leaves lying beneath the plane trees.

'I thought we'd go to The Pentagram?' Ryan Falconer suggested casually.

The Pentagram was rated as one of London's top restaurants, but walking on air just to be with this fascinating stranger Virginia wouldn't have cared if they'd gone to the burger bar.

'If that's all right with you?' he added politely.

'It sounds wonderful, but...'

'But?'

'I'm not sure if I'm well enough dressed,' she admitted a shade awkwardly.

Glancing at her off-the-peg aubergine suit and cream blouse, he said, 'You look fine to me.'

A black executive-type limousine was drawn up a short distance away. As they approached, the liveried chauffeur jumped out and held open the door.

Feeling rather like a latter-day Cinderella, Virginia was handed in. After a brief word with the chauffeur, Ryan Falconer slid in beside her, and a moment later the sleek car drew away from the kerb and into the traffic stream.

Turning his head, he smiled at her. A smile that set her pulses hammering, and made her feel suddenly, unaccountably breathless.

He was so close, his physical presence so overwhelming, that she felt as dizzy and disorientated as if she was sitting perched on the edge of a precipice.

Yet, her perceptions heightened, she registered the length of his lashes, the way his ears were set neatly against his dark head, the shallow cleft in his strong chin, the little creases each side of his mouth that deepened when he smiled...

Becoming aware that she was staring at him as though mesmerised, she dragged her gaze away, and felt herself go hot all over.

His lips twitched and, certain that he could guess exactly how she felt, she said as coolly as possible, 'You mentioned there was something you'd like to discuss with me?'

'There is,' he agreed, 'but it'll keep until after lunch.'

With a faint recollection that The Pentagram was somewhere on the other side of town, she queried, 'How long will it take to get to the restaurant?'

'About twenty minutes,' he answered casually.

Twenty minutes! 'Mr Falconer, I'm not sure if there's time to—'

'Ryan,' he insisted. 'And don't worry, there's plenty of time. Mrs Trantor gave you the rest of the afternoon off.'

'The rest of the afternoon off?' she echoed in amazement. 'How on earth did you persuade her to do that?'

He grimaced ruefully. 'And here I was, hoping you'd put it all down to charm.'

Remembering Mrs Trantor's face, she said, 'I'm sure charm had a lot to do with it.'

'Not half as much as the thought of doing business with me. All I had to do was mention that I was looking to buy a Jonathan Cass.'

She blinked. If he was 'looking to buy' one of Jonathan Cass's paintings, apart from the fact that he couldn't be short of a million or two, that put him straight into the connoisseur class.

'Then, you're a lover of art?'

He considered that. 'More a businessman. As far as art's concerned, I buy whatever will make a profit, unless it's for my own private collection. In that case I buy only the things I like.'

'Is the Cass…?'

'For my own collection. Though I may hang it in the gallery for a while to promote interest.'

'You have a gallery?'

'On Madison Avenue. That's the reason I know your parents. They put on a joint exhibition there a few weeks ago.

'Tell me something, Virginia…may I call you Virginia?'

She nodded. 'Of course.'

'Why didn't you tell the Trantors that your parents are Brad and Mia Adams?'

'I didn't think it was relevant.' Then, quickly, she asked, 'How do you know I didn't tell them?'

'It's quite obvious. If they knew, they wouldn't be treating you like some glorified receptionist.'

'Unfortunately at the present that's what I am.'

'How long have you been at the gallery?'

'Almost four months.'

He frowned. 'Why stay? You surely didn't spend those years at college just to sit behind a desk and answer inane questions?'

'No, I didn't. But jobs in the art world aren't that easy to come by.'

'More doors would be open to you if you made it known who your parents are.'

She shook her head stubbornly. 'Particularly as I have no *creative* talent, who my parents are shouldn't make any difference. What I've learnt and am capable of, should.'

'I totally agree, but I still think you're making it hard for yourself.'

'No, I'm just refusing to make it easy.'

She saw the mingled respect and admiration in his eyes, before he remarked, 'You know, you're really quite exceptional. Most people would use every trick in the book to gain an advantage...

'But, then, I hadn't expected you to be like most people. With talented parents like yours—' Breaking off, he added firmly, 'And I don't mean that in the way you're thinking.'

A little stiffly, she asked, 'How do you mean it?'

He turned those extraordinary eyes on her, making butterflies dance in her stomach, before continuing obliquely, 'I imagine it wasn't easy being brought up by two such art-absorbed people?'

Without waiting for an answer, he went on, 'I gather you were an only child, so you must often have felt lonely and neglected?'

'Yes, I did,' she admitted. And found herself telling him something that, up until then, she had never told another living soul. 'I had everything I needed as far as material things went, but they never had any time for me, never sat me on their knees or cuddled me.'

'I guess people who live for art, or have any other overwhelming interest, for that matter, tend to disregard their children.'

'You sound as if you speak from personal experience.'

He smiled wryly. 'I guess we're two of a kind. Though I had everything that money could buy, until I was nearly ten the only thing I knew about love was how to live without it.'

Understanding exactly how he'd felt, her heart went out to the forlorn little boy he must have been.

Reading her sympathy, he took her hand and gave it a little squeeze, making her heart turn over, before going on, 'My father's two main interests in life were making money and politics. He spent most of his time either on Wall Street, or attending political rallies, so I saw hardly anything of him.

'That wouldn't have mattered quite so much if my mother had made time for me. But she too had an absorbing passion for politics.

'If she wasn't actively campaigning or fund-raising, most of her time was devoted to playing hostess at glittering social occasions, where she could hobnob with past and, hopefully, future presidents.

'Once she had reluctantly provided my father with the son and heir he needed, I was given over to the care of nannies, and later, various tutors...'

A strange sensation came over her as she watched his face and listened. She *knew* this man as if his soul was a mirror image of her own... But that was just being fanciful, she told herself firmly. Yet the feeling that he was the other half of herself persisted.

'I was almost ten when she was killed in a plane crash,' Ryan went on. 'But I'd seen so little of her, that after a few months I could hardly remember what she looked like.

'It was only when my father remarried that I discovered what real care and warmth felt like.

'Beth, an English widow with a young son and baby daughter from a previous marriage, always had time for me.

She took me to her heart and gave me all the love I'd lacked up until then... Ah, here we are...'

They had drawn up in a quiet, tree-lined street in front of a handsome porticoed building that looked more like a private house than a restaurant. Only the five-pointed star and the name in gold letters above the door identified it.

'I'm sorry,' he apologised, as he helped her out.

'For what?' she asked, puzzled.

'My intention was to talk about you. Instead I've bored you stiff talking about myself.'

Shaking her head, she said, 'I haven't been in the least bit bored.'

'You're either very nicely mannered or a diplomat. I'll be able to judge which when I get to know you better.'

The suggestion that he intended to get to know her better had her walking on cloud nine as they made their way into an elegant marble-floored foyer.

'Mr Falconer... How nice to see you again.'

They were greeted by the dapper, silver-haired manager, a cream rosebud in his buttonhole.

'Nice to see you, Michael.'

The two men shook hands.

'Are you over for long?'

'A few days.'

'Then, perhaps we'll see you again?'

'I certainly hope so.'

Alerted by a discreet beep, the manager said, 'It seems I'm wanted. Please excuse me. Alphonse will show you to your table.'

Rubbing his hands together, he gave Virginia a little bow, and departed at a trot.

The *maître d'*, appearing like a genie from a lamp, led them through to a dining-room with a rich Turkish carpet and a crimson and gold decor.

There were eight widely spaced tables, six of which were already occupied, and at the far end of the room several small velvet covered couches were grouped cosily around a blazing log fire.

Their table, covered by a spotless damask cloth and set with fine crystal and a centrepiece of cream rosebuds, was by one of the long windows.

As soon as Virginia was seated, the *maître d'* disappeared, and a younger waiter appeared with two glasses of pale amber sherry on a silver tray.

'I hope you like dry sherry?' Ryan asked in a stage whisper, as the man departed.

'Yes, I do.'

'Every single thing that's served here is of the finest, which makes it a rewarding experience, but there's no choice.'

'You mean no one knows what they're getting until it arrives?'

Making it into a game, he said, 'Not unless you ask, which counts as being chicken, or peek at another table, which is frowned on.'

Almost certain he was pulling her leg, she said serenely, 'Well, there's not much I don't like...'

'I do admire a woman with a spirit of adventure.'

'Apart from fresh oysters,' she tacked on.

His dark eyes gleamed between their long thick lashes. 'Oysters are something of a speciality here.'

She barely repressed a shudder.

'I hope I'm not making you nervous?' he enquired innocently.

'Not at all,' she lied, adding, 'if the worst comes to the worst I can always leave them.'

'Not if you want to get out of here alive.'

Certain now that he was pulling her leg, she smiled, a lovely smile that showed her white, even teeth, dimpled the corners of her mouth, and made her grey-green eyes dance.

Softly, he said, 'You're quite enchanting when you smile.' Then watching a tinge of pink appear along her cheekbones, he said, 'I thought that went out with the Victorians.'

'What went out with the Victorians?'

A little amused smile tugging at his lips, he told her, 'The ability to blush at a compliment. I find it most...refreshing.'

Ruffled by that smile, she snapped, 'Don't you mean *entertaining*?'

'That too, but in the nicest possible way,' he agreed, refusing to be put out by her tart tone.

Fighting back, she said, 'Well blushing is the only piece in my repertoire, so don't expect me to get the vapours, or scream if I see a mouse.'

'If you see a mouse here I'm the one who's likely to do the screaming,' he said humorously.

As she stared at him in disbelief, he explained, 'It wouldn't do much for the reputation of the place, and as I've a stake in it...'

'A stake in it? I thought you lived in New York.'

'So I do, but as an international investment banker I've got a finger in a lot of pies.'

As he finished speaking, a seafood torte arrived, accompanied by a chilled white wine.

'Okay?' Ryan queried.

'Fine, thank you,' Virginia answered politely. She soon discovered it was more than fine. It was absolutely delicious.

With impeccable timing, the torte was followed by a cheese soufflé, incredibly tasty and as light as air, and a fruit compote with Madeira. A small sorbet was served between each course.

It would have been sacrilege to talk, and neither spoke as they savoured the superb meal, but Virginia was heart-stoppingly conscious that Ryan's eyes were more often on her face than his plate.

Only when coffee had been served and they had moved to sit in front of the fire, did he ask laconically, 'Well?'

'That was a totally new experience,' she admitted.

'And?'

'You were right about it being a rewarding one.'

'I'm glad you think so. Incidentally, I've just had a new experience.'

When she looked at him enquiringly, he told her, 'You're the first woman I've brought here who hasn't chattered non-stop throughout the meal.'

She was wondering if he thought her dull company, when he added, 'Who was it who called his wife, My gracious silence?'

'I don't know,' she admitted, feeling a little glow of pleasure at his words. Though they had only just met, his approval meant a lot to her.

Stretching long legs towards the fire, he queried, 'Tell me, Virginia, have you ever been to New York?'

Somewhat thrown by the sudden change of subject, she answered, 'No, but I've always wanted to.'

He nodded as if satisfied, before asking, 'How would you like to work there?'

'I'd love to, but...' Then, uncertainly, she asked, 'Are you offering me a job?'

'Don't you want one?'

With a sudden suspicion, she said, 'It depends on why you're offering it.'

'You think it's because of your parents?'

'Isn't it?'

'Earlier you said, "Who my parents are shouldn't make any difference. What I've learnt and am capable of, should." I go along with that.'

His dark brows drawn together in a frown, he added, 'Do you honestly believe that as far as I'm concerned, it matters one iota who your parents are?'

Feeling foolish, she said, 'But presumably they must

have mentioned me? Otherwise you would never have known I existed.'

'I'm not denying that we talked about you.'

'I can't imagine why,' she said flatly. 'It's over three months since I heard from them.'

'They seemed very proud of what you had achieved. I understand you got some special student award?'

'Yes.'

'For what, exactly?'

'The assignment was to set up from scratch an exhibition by an unknown artist.'

'What did that involve?'

'Putting into practice everything I'd learnt about selecting canvases, framing, lighting, printing techniques, cataloguing, publicity, etc. The main thing of course, was to make the show a success financially as well as critically.'

'Did you enjoy it?'

'Very much.'

'Would you like to do the same thing on a regular basis?'

Trying to hide the rush of excitement, she asked carefully, 'Is that the job you're offering me?'

'Yes.'

'Why?'

'Because my assistant curator, Miss Caulfield, who has been with me for the past four years, is leaving to get married. Her future husband is Canadian, and they're moving to Vancouver to live.'

'I mean, why me? There must be any number of more experienced people who would be only too pleased to take a post like that.'

He shrugged. 'I dare say that's true, but I've always believed in giving new blood a chance.'

Speaking her thoughts aloud, she said, 'It sounds fantastic, but I'd need somewhere to live.'

'There's an apartment that goes with the job, which incidentally carries a salary of—'

He named a figure that to Virginia seemed astronomical and, apparently reading her surprise, went on, 'It isn't cheap to live in New York, but I think you'll enjoy it.'

He spoke as if she had already accepted, she noted dazedly and, while she found it hard to believe that a man like Ryan Falconer had gone out of his way to look her up and offer her such an opportunity, she was choked by excitement.

It was a chance in a million. Not only would she be going to live in one of the most exciting cities in the world and doing the very job she wanted to do, but she would be working for him...

Though was that a good thing? the voice of caution asked. She was already dangerously smitten, and a man of that age, a man as attractive as Ryan, would almost certainly be either married, or involved in a long-term relationship.

But even if by some miracle he was neither, she was just an ordinary working girl, and therefore way out of his league. If she allowed her feelings to run away with her, she could get badly hurt. So would it be sensible to accept his very tempting offer?

Even while she asked herself the question, she knew in her heart of hearts that it would be anything but... And she was no risk-taker...

He broke the lengthening silence to ask quietly, 'But perhaps you feel you can't accept my offer because of your parents' involvement, slight though it was?'

'No, I—'

'I can assure you they didn't try to sell you...'

She could believe it. They didn't care about her enough to do that.

'In fact, though they told me where to find you, they haven't the faintest idea that I was even thinking of offering you a job...'

Then with the slightest hint of impatience, carefully controlled, he asked, 'So what do you say?'

Knowing quite well that she should refuse, she threw caution to the winds, and said eagerly, 'Yes, thank you, I'll take it.'

He smiled, and just for a moment she could have sworn he looked immensely relieved. But she must have misread his expression...

Holding out his hand he suggested lightly, 'Well, now you've made your decision, let's shake on it.'

With a strange feeling of going to meet her fate, she put her hand into his, and felt a little tingle of electricity run right up her arm.

His physical effect on her was devastating, and common sense warned her she was playing with fire. But, she realised with a sense of inevitability, she was already too deeply involved to care.

Her practical streak kicking in, and wondering how long it would take to save the air fare, she asked, 'When would you want me to start?'

'As soon as possible. Next week, preferably.'

'Oh...'

'Don't worry, I'll tell the Trantors you won't be going back, and make it right with them.'

'It's not just that,' she began awkwardly.

'There's some other complication?' His tone sharpened. 'A boyfriend perhaps?'

'No. At least no one serious.'

His manner growing relaxed once more, he said, 'You mentioned having a furnished flat... It's rented, presumably?'

'Yes.'

'So that presents no problem... I hope you're not one of the people who loathe flying?'

'No. At least I don't think so. I've never really flown anywhere.'

'But you do have a passport?'

'Yes. Just before I left college I went travelling with a group of other students in a ramshackle bus that broke down almost every day.'

'Sounds like fun.'

'It was.' She smiled at the memory.

Watching her face, and thinking how exquisite she was, he asked, 'So what exactly is the difficulty?'

'I'm afraid I haven't the money for the air fare,' she admitted reluctantly.

'My dear Virginia, I don't expect you to pay your own air fare. In fact I'd planned to take you back with me on the company jet.'

Bemused, she thought it sounded more as if he'd mounted a determined campaign to get her, rather than merely offering her a job opportunity. But perhaps that was how these high-powered American businessmen talked?

'Can you be ready to travel by Friday?'

Today was Wednesday. Apart from notifying her landlord that she was leaving, and packing her few personal belongings, there was little to do.

'Yes, I can be ready.'

'Good.'

Curiosity overcoming her innate shyness, she asked, 'What would have happened if I'd said I couldn't?'

He smiled. 'I would have put the jet on hold.'

Seeing how staggered she looked, he added in that ironic, self-mocking way she was starting to get to know, 'I'm the boss, and getting what I want is the name of the game.'

CHAPTER FOUR

THE company jet, though looking small against the commercial giants, was the height of luxury, with its own chef, a well-fitted *en-suite* bedroom, and a Monet hanging in the lounge.

Their flight across the pond, as the pilot called it, was smooth and uneventful but as far as Virginia was concerned, given the circumstances, it was the most thrilling thing she had ever done in her life.

Not that she'd done that much, she admitted, when Ryan, noting her suppressed excitement, teased her about it.

When they reached John F. Kennedy airport, a silver chauffeur-driven limousine was waiting to take them into the city.

'Though the birds-eye views are striking,' Ryan told her, 'I decided against the helicopter. Beth, who remembers driving into town for the first time, says it's an experience that shouldn't be missed.'

As far as Virginia was concerned even that was an understatement. New York, with its soaring buildings and superb skyline, was everything she had expected and more. A city by the sea, it had a luminous quality of light she hadn't even begun to envisage.

She felt she should pinch herself, but was afraid to in case she woke up. If this was a dream, she never wanted it to end.

Since taking her to The Pentagram, Ryan had scarcely left her side. No lover could have been more attentive.

When she had hesitantly asked if he hadn't something more important to do, he'd answered with a grin, 'The most important thing is making sure you don't change your mind.'

Why was it important that she shouldn't change her mind? she had wondered. Or had it been just a light, meaningless remark?

Probably.

Still he showed every sign of wanting her company, and for the past two evenings had insisted on taking her out to dinner. Each time he had delivered her safely back to her flat at a most respectable hour.

She had warned herself repeatedly that it would be madness to fall in love with him, until it was borne upon her that it was already too late.

Totally enslaved, liking him as well as loving him, all her usual rules of conduct had flown out of the window and, having discovered that he had neither a wife nor a current lady friend, if he had asked to stay, she would have found it difficult to refuse.

But he didn't. And the sensible part of her was grateful. It would have been the height of stupidity to get involved with a man like Ryan.

Yet she was already involved, emotionally if not physically, and had been since the moment he'd walked into the gallery.

Already, with no guarantee of it lasting, she would have sold her soul to be in his arms.

A truly modern woman might have made the first move, but she wasn't the type. She had neither the courage nor the confidence. Indeed, in the circumstances, a kind of perverse pride forbade it.

Apart from anything else, he might not be interested in her as a woman.

Though on more than one occasion she had glimpsed a little flame in those indigo eyes that had set her pulses racing, and had made her think the attraction might be mutual.

Still, so long as Ryan held back, she was safe.

But while he'd made no attempt to deepen the relationship, his attitude couldn't be called businesslike. He treated her with a kind of quixotic, self-mocking camaraderie, that at once pleased and puzzled her.

She couldn't bring herself to believe that he treated all his prospective employees in that way, so what made her different?

Though it seemed to make no sense, the only reason she could come up with was her parents. Not wanting to rock the boat, however, she had said nothing.

The traffic was very heavy as they drove into town, and it was late afternoon by the time they reached Fifth Avenue, with its bustling pedestrians, its spectacular buildings, and brilliantly lit shop windows.

All the colours of the rainbow seemed to be reflected in the towering glass skyscrapers, while in Central Park the trees glowed gold and bronze and scarlet in the last dying rays of the sun.

Well used to keeping her emotions hidden, for once in her life Virginia was unable to do so. Fascinated by the beauty and vibrancy of that famous avenue, its air of being *en fête*, she exclaimed, 'Isn't it wonderful?'

Ryan smiled. 'Then, you won't mind living here?'

Thinking he meant the city, she exclaimed, 'I'm sure I'll love it.'

Then, eagerly, she asked 'Where exactly will I be living?' Somehow, in the excitement and upheaval of the last forty eight hours, it was something she hadn't got round to asking.

'Here.'

'Here? You surely don't mean on Fifth Avenue?'

'I do mean on Fifth Avenue,' he contradicted. 'In fact in this very building,' he added, as they drew up outside a skyscraper with glittering window displays each side of an imposing entrance.

'It's known as Falconer's Tower. It was built just over thirty years ago when my father decided to put some of the profits from his investment in paper mills into real estate...'

While the smart young chauffeur opened the door and stood rigidly to attention, Ryan handed Virginia out and, hiding a slight smile, said gravely, 'Thank you, Carlson. Will you have the luggage sent straight up?'

'Certainly, Mr Falconer.'

Craning her neck to peer up at the glass tower, Virginia said, 'It's so tall. How on earth do you fill so much space?'

'There's a car park below the shopping mall and, above, office and business accommodation. Next comes a comprehensive leisure complex. Then the top two floors are divided into four separate apartments.

'I'm living in the penthouse at the moment...' Watching her face, he added deliberately, 'You have the small apartment next door.'

As she gaped at him, a hand beneath her elbow, he escorted her across the sidewalk and into a chandelier-hung private lobby, where a stocky, middle-aged security guard gave them a laconic salute.

'Afternoon, Mr Falconer.'

'Afternoon George. How's the new son and heir?'

Beaming proudly, George answered, 'Fine. Just fine. Starting to look like his old dad.'

'Could do worse. By the way, this is Miss Adams. She'll be living upstairs.'

'Right, Mr Falconer. I'll let the others know.'

While the elevator whisked them smoothly upwards, Virginia tried to catch her breath. She had expected a single room 'walk-up' in one of the less salubrious areas. In her wildest dreams she had never imagined living on Fifth Avenue next door to Ryan.

The whole thing was incredible. It made no sense. He wasn't treating her like an employee at all. And once again she wondered, why not?

But maybe his present assistant curator was still occupying the apartment that went with the job?

'Is this a temporary arrangement?' she queried.

He slanted her a glance. 'What makes you ask?'

Then instantly on her wavelength, he said, 'Oh, I see. No, it isn't temporary. The building where Miss Caulfield is living now has been earmarked for redevelopment, and as the unit next to mine happened to be standing empty...'

Why was an apartment in such a prestigious building standing empty? she wondered.

As though reading her thoughts, he explained, 'We had expected Janice, my stepsister, to move into it when she finished college, but she's changed her mind about staying in New York.'

A twinkle in his eye, he added, 'It may have something to do with a handsome young diplomat who, in a month or so, is returning to Washington. In the meantime she's keeping Beth company...'

As he finished speaking the elevator sighed to a halt and the doors slid open.

They emerged into a spacious, marble-floored foyer, where ornamental trees in tubs were interspersed with statues of Greek gods.

'A bit over the top, don't you think?' Ryan asked, pulling a face. 'Apparently it was my mother's idea and, as I'd just been born, my father decided to indulge her whim. However, I've always loved this.' Above a central staircase, a huge round window provided a dramatic view over the roof tops. 'I used to call it my sky window.'

On the opposite wall, there was a series of smaller matching inner windows on either side of a large handsomely carved door.

'That's the penthouse suite. It was the main family home when my father was alive. In those days he and Beth did a lot of entertaining.

'But after he died, a couple of years back, Beth, who

had suffered a mild heart attack, decided to move out. She wanted somewhere smaller and cosier...

'And this is where you'll be living.' He steered Virginia to a slightly more modest-looking door on the left and, having opened it, led the way inside. 'Let me show you around. As I said, this apartment's quite small, but it is on the corner of the building, so you get good views in both directions...'

Feeling rather like Alice in Wonderland, she left her shoulder bag in the hall and followed him, only to discover that her 'quite small' apartment was much bigger and grander than she could ever have imagined.

Though it had only one bedroom, that and the other three rooms, a living-room, a dining-room, and a well-stocked kitchen, were large and airy and luxuriously furnished.

Both outer walls of the living-room had sliding glass panels that opened onto a pleasant terrace and roof-garden with views that, rather than merely good, Virginia would have called fantastic.

The sun had gone down now leaving the sky streaked with pink and plum and palest green, while all over the city a myriad of lights were starting to spangle the encroaching dusk.

'Like it?' Ryan asked.

Speechless, she nodded.

'When you've had a chance to relax and settle in I'll take you to Clouds for dinner.'

Clouds, she knew, was equally famous as the Rainbow Room.

Her cup was running over, when he added casually, 'On the way out we'll stop so you can meet the rest of the family.'

Somehow she found her voice. 'The rest of the family?'

'Beth and Janice have an apartment on the floor below, and my stepbrother, Steven, and his wife Madeline, live next door to them.'

So she would be living surrounded by the whole of the Falconer clan, Virginia thought dazedly.

'They're expecting us to call in, so they'll all be assembled. Don't worry, it's not as bad as it sounds,' he added cheerfully. 'None of them actually bite, and I'm sure you'll like Beth...'

It was obvious from the way his face softened that he was very fond of his stepmother.

As she followed him back to the hall, he added, 'In fact I hope and believe you'll all get on well together.'

Seeing he was waiting for a response, and sensing that for some reason it was important to him, she said with more conviction than she felt, 'I'm sure we will.'

If that was what Ryan wanted, no matter what happened, she would do her best to get on well with them.

But how would they feel about it?

It was clear from what he'd said previously that they were a family who moved in wealthy upper-class New York society circles, who mingled with presidents and the like.

While she, though she had had the benefit of a good education, was a virtual nobody to them, who worked for a living. And what was worse, she was Ryan's employee...

The bell rang, breaking into her uneasy musings.

'This will be the luggage,' Ryan remarked and, opening the door, directed a blue-uniformed youth with a trolley. 'Leave those two pieces, Rawdon will deal with them. The other two need to come in here... Where would you like them?' He raised an interrogative eyebrow at Virginia. 'The bedroom?'

'Please.' She tried to sound crisp and businesslike.

When Ryan had first shown her the bedroom, the sight of the big double bed and the erotic images it had immediately conjured up, had made her blush.

Catching his eye, and guessing by the gleam in it that

he had been following her train of thought, she had blushed even harder and had hurried out.

As soon as the cases had been deposited, some dollar bills changed hands, and with a chirpy, 'Thanks, Mr Falconer,' the youth departed.

Standing by the open door, Ryan said, 'Well, I'll leave you to unpack and make yourself at home... Oh, and you'll need this.' He dropped the latch key into her hand.

'Thank you.'

Suddenly, and perhaps for the first time, the whole thing seemed real. For better or worse she was here in New York, starting a new and thrilling job, living on Fifth Avenue, next door to Ryan...

She smiled up at him, her face reflecting all the excitement and anticipation, the gladness and joy of being here with him.

Making no move to go, he stood looking down at her radiant face, his own face strangely taut.

When he bent his head slightly, she thought for one heart-stopping moment that he was about to kiss her.

Instead, he touched her cheek with a single finger, sending a frisson of pleasure running through her. 'It's been a long day and you'll probably need an early night, so I'll call for you about seven.'

While she stood like a statue, he went out, closing the door quietly behind him.

Rooted to the spot, it was a little while before she could pull herself together enough to head for the bedroom.

Only when she approached her cases to start unpacking did she realise she was still holding the key Ryan had given her, clutching it so hard that it had made a white imprint in her soft palm.

It was just before seven when the doorbell rang. Wearing the only cocktail dress he hadn't seen and, after taking a lot of time and trouble, satisfied she was looking her best, Virginia went to answer.

Dressed in a well-cut dinner jacket and stylish shirt, his thick dark hair curling a little, Ryan stood smiling down at her, making her pulses race and her knees grow weak.

As well as being breathtakingly handsome, he looked so cool and self-assured, that her small reservoir of confidence evaporated on the spot, and she found herself asking anxiously, 'Will I do?'

He looked her over from head to toe, taking in her glossy ash-brown hair, her lovely face with its greeny-grey eyes and wide, passionate mouth, her slender figure in the simple green sheath, her lack of jewellery, and thought he'd never seen anything more beautiful.

Raising her hand to his lips, he kissed the palm.

The romantic little gesture took her breath away.

'There won't be a man there who doesn't envy me,' he assured her.

Watching her long lashes sweep down and a tinge of pink come into her cheeks, he felt such a surge of desire that his voice was almost rough as he asked, 'Have you a coat?'

She produced a soft fun-fur jacket which he helped her into, before suggesting, 'As the family live only one floor below, shall we walk down?'

All her previous apprehension returning, she nodded, trying unsuccessfully to hide her nervousness.

With a reassuring smile, he tucked her hand through his arm, and together they descended the marble staircase to a foyer no less impressive than the one they had just left.

Ryan had barely touched the bell of the nearest door when it opened, giving the impression that the occupant had been waiting with some eagerness.

'You must be Miss Adams. Do come in.' A smiling, silver-haired woman drew Virginia into a charming hallway. 'I'm Elizabeth Falconer, Ryan's stepmother...'

There was no sign of the cool standoffishness that Virginia had dreaded, in fact just the opposite.

'But please call me Beth, if you'd care to. Almost everyone does…'

Elizabeth Falconer who, after more than twenty years in the States, still spoke with an English accent, was short and slender, with soft brown eyes and a pretty, gentle face.

She had an unmistakable air of warmth and generosity, which marked her as a woman who loved more than she hated, and gave more than she took.

Virginia liked her on sight.

'Come through and meet the rest of the family.'

There were three people in the large attractive living-room.

A striking blonde in her early thirties was sitting on the couch, a magazine open on her knee.

Standing by a built-in bar, a pleasant-looking man of medium height, with fairish hair and blue eyes, was serving drinks.

And perched on a pouffe in front of an open fire, a regal-looking tortoiseshell cat on her lap, was a young woman with below shoulder-length dark hair.

'Jump down, Sheba.' Pushing the affronted cat off, the girl scrambled to her feet and came to meet them.

'This is my daughter, Janice,' Beth Falconer said fondly.

With the same gentle face, the same brown eyes, and the same petite build, Janice was a carbon copy of her mother.

'Hi!' she said with a friendly smile. 'So you're Virginia.' Then cryptically, she added, 'Ryan was right.'

'And this is my son, Steven,' Beth went on.

Though the eye-colour was different, there was no mistaking the family likeness as Steven came forward to shake hands warmly. 'It's very nice to meet you, Miss Adams… Or do you mind if I call you Virginia?'

'I hope you will.' Virginia's smile held both relief and pleasure, and encompassed them all.

With obvious pride, Steven went on, 'May I introduce my wife, Madeline.'

His pride was fully justified. A natural blonde, with a stunning figure and long slender legs, Madeline was one of the most beautiful women Virginia had ever seen.

'Hello, Miss Adams.' The aquamarine eyes surveyed her coolly. 'Are you nicely settled in? I must admit we were all rather stunned when Ryan said he was bringing a woman he'd only just met back with him.'

The words and the accompanying smile were, on the surface, civil enough but, sensing an underlying hint of censure, Virginia said, 'I'm sure you must have been. Everything has happened so quickly that I still feel that way myself.'

'Won't you take off your coat and sit down?'

'What can I get you to drink?'

Steven and his mother spoke simultaneously.

Before Virginia could respond to either, Ryan, who had been standing quietly in the background, said firmly, 'Thanks, but Carlson will have the car waiting. We're dining at Clouds. I booked a table for seven thirty as Virginia will need an early night.'

'I'm quite sure you both will,' Madeline murmured sweetly.

Accompanying them to the door, Beth gave Ryan a little smile and patted his arm, as though in tacit approval.

Then, turning to Virginia, she urged, 'As we're so close, do pop in any time. You'll be very welcome... By the way, I've tried to make sure you have enough supplies to last until you get sorted out, but if there's anything else you need just let me know.'

'Thank you, you're very kind,' Virginia said, and meant it.

'Not too much of an ordeal, was it?' Ryan asked as the elevator carried them downwards.

'Not at all. They couldn't have been nicer.'

'Madeline could,' he said bluntly. 'But then, I should have expected it. She's not one to make friends with other women, particularly beautiful ones.'

Startled, Virginia protested, 'But I'm not beautiful.'

He turned his head to smile at her. 'That's a matter of opinion. I think you are.'

Even if she didn't think so, she found herself walking on air because he thought her so.

Clouds, with its live orchestra and gleaming dance floor, its rich ambience and even richer clientele, was out of this world.

Almost literally.

One of the highest restaurants in Manhattan, it had magical views over the jewel-encrusted city. A city that, like a beautiful woman, only truly came into its own at night.

But for all the wealth of wonder outside, Virginia's eyes were more often on the man who sat opposite her at their small table.

To begin with she made an effort to be practical, to ask about the gallery and the job she would soon be starting, but Ryan shook his head at her.

'This is no time to be talking about work. We're here to relax and enjoy ourselves. Okay?'

'Okay.'

Embracing the here and now, and refusing to allow the future and what kind of problems it might hold, to dim her happiness, she gave herself up to the sheer delight of being with Ryan in such a marvellous venue.

The evening flew as they talked and laughed, drank fine wine, and ate delicious food, which, head-over-heels in love, she scarcely tasted.

Ryan was a charming and stimulating companion who struck sparks off her and made her feel wittier and more glamorous than she knew herself to be.

But as well as the razzle-dazzle there was a sense of harmony between them, a feeling of rightness and contentment, as if they were both exactly where they wanted to be.

By the time the coffee was served, however, beneath the surface ease was a growing tension, a sexual awareness that made her unable to meet his eyes, and caused her first to stumble over words, and then lapse into silence.

'More coffee?' Ryan asked.

'No, thank you.'

'Would you like to stay and dance for a while...?'

Just the thought of being held in his arms made her tremble and turned her insides to jelly.

'Or perhaps you're ready to go?'

Unworldly though she was, she knew he was asking a great deal more than that simple question, and what she answered was crucial.

Once she had burnt her bridges, there could be no turning back. So was it the employer, or the man, who really mattered?

Certainly the man.

But suppose he just wanted a one-night stand? Or, at the most, a brief fling? Could she live with that? The loss of pride? The possible humiliation?

The problem was she didn't know him well enough to be certain what kind of man he was beneath that charming exterior.

Some men could be cold-blooded and calculating. What if she proved to be just an embarrassment to him once he'd got what he wanted?

She could end up with no job, no money, nowhere to live, and no way of getting home.

The possibilities were dire.

But somehow none of it seemed to matter.

It was as though the whole thing had been preordained. As though they had been destined to meet and become lovers...

While the thoughts raced through her mind, he sat quietly watching her face.

Though he showed no outward sign, she sensed his impatience and, her own suddenly matching it, said thickly, 'Yes, I'm ready to go.'

While he paid the bill, her coat was produced, Carlson was alerted, and a minute later they were going down in the elevator, standing carefully apart.

The limousine was waiting, and they drove back in silence, keeping a good foot of space between them, as though afraid to touch in case the conflagration started.

When they reached Falconer's Tower, Ryan said goodnight to Carlson and paused to have a word with the night security guard, his leisurely air belying the need that was driving him.

In the elevator, he took Virginia's hand and, feeling her tremble, said, 'I hadn't meant to rush you, but I find I can't help myself.'

Then with a scrupulousness she could only admire, 'You do want this, don't you?'

'Yes,' she whispered.

'Sure?'

'Quite sure.'

He bent his dark head and kissed her.

During her years at college she had gone out with a number of would-be boyfriends and had been kissed many times.

At worst, they had been hot and wet and faintly nauseating, causing her to break off that particular encounter without delay. At best, they had been pleasant. But even the pleasant ones had never stirred her enough to make her want to repeat the experience.

Ryan's kiss, on the other hand, filled her with a soaring wonder and delight that melted every bone in her body and left her hungry for more.

As the elevator slid to a halt and the doors opened, she

found herself wondering briefly which apartment he would choose to take her to.

Probably hers.

Using his own seemed to *commit* him more. Added to that, he no doubt had a staff of servants to complicate matters.

Still holding her hand, he led her across the lobby to his penthouse.

'What about the servants?' she asked huskily.

'There's only Rawdon, and he's very discreet. He has his own quarters, and stays there unless I buzz for him.'

Opening the door, he swept her into his arms and, using his heel to close the door behind them, carried her through to the bedroom.

Setting her down gently, he slipped off her coat and shoes and, his eyes dark and intent, began to undress her.

Though there was an urgency that wouldn't be denied, his hands were deft as he removed her stockings; and he unfastened her bra without fumbling.

As soon as she was naked, he laid her on the bed and gazed his fill, before stripping off his own clothes.

Broad across the shoulders and narrow-hipped, his limbs perfectly in proportion, he was magnificent, and her breath caught her throat at the sight of him.

He carried not an ounce of surplus weight, and muscles rippled beneath a smooth, tanned skin as he leaned down to kiss her.

Then, a man claiming his mate with a kind of triumphant certainty, he lowered himself into the waiting cradle of her hips.

Poised for an instant, hard male flesh against female softness, he smiled into her eyes while she gazed back at him.

Though she wanted him with every fibre of her being, she gasped at his first strong thrust. But the brief pain was unimportant, swept away in the heat and rapture of their coming together.

The first driving need over, amazed and pleased by the fact that she had been a virgin, he made love to her again.

This time he took it slowly.

As well as using a leisurely and skilful expertise that lifted her to heights of ecstasy she had never even dreamt of, he made love to her with words, telling her how exquisite her breasts were, how flawless her skin was, how much she delighted him.

She was still quivering with pleasure when he lifted himself away and, gathering her close, settled her head on his shoulder.

His hand stroking up and down her arm, he said softly, wonderingly, 'You're such a joy to make love to. Not only are you the most beautiful woman I've ever seen, but you respond with such warmth and passion. I can't understand how you've managed to stay a virgin this long.'

Feeling like an oddity, she said, 'It wasn't intentional. Somehow it just happened...'

Naturally discriminating, she had avoided the more obvious pitfalls of adolescence until maturity had helped her to value herself as a woman.

'I didn't like the idea of casual sex, and I never met a man I cared for enough to sleep with.' Too late she realised how revealing that last sentence was.

'Does that mean you care for me?' he asked tenderly.

Somehow, she answered, 'It means I find you attractive.'

'Is that all?'

'Isn't that enough?'

'I hardly think so. You see, I want to marry you.'

'Marry me?' She sounded as staggered as she felt.

'Marry you,' he repeated firmly.

Convinced that this must be some kind of leg-pull, she said, 'Hadn't you better be careful? I might take you seriously.'

'I *want* you to take me seriously.'

'You can't mean you really *do* want to marry me.'

'It's hardly the kind of thing I'd joke about.'

'But we've only just met.'

'Don't you believe in love at first sight?'

'Yes...' Having lost her heart to him the moment she had set eyes on him, she could hardly deny it.

His hand moved to take her chin and lift her face to his. 'I was rather hoping you did.'

'B-but we're poles apart,' she stammered. 'You're—'

'A man who wants to marry you.' Dropping a kiss on her nose, he added quizzically, 'I must say you're taking an awful lot of convincing.'

'I don't understand why you want to marry me. Most people these days just opt for a relationship.'

'Is that what you want?'

'No,' she admitted.

He kissed her. 'Me neither. I guess I've just got old-fashioned values. Finding my future wife has too, is an unexpected pleasure.'

My future wife...

Much as she wanted to believe it was possible, she was still troubled by their differing backgrounds.

'Another reason for getting married is that in a year or two's time I'd like to have children and I want them with you. Wouldn't you like a family?'

'Yes, I would.'

Watching her face, he asked, 'So what's bothering you?'

'Our lifestyles are so dissimilar.'

'But not incompatible. Don't you think you could get used to being rich?'

'It's not just that. It's the whole thing. You live in a completely different world. Move in a different society...'

'You're living in my world now, and the society I move in would welcome you with open arms. You're beautiful, intelligent, well-educated; you have character and style—'

'And famous parents?'

'Not to mention a chip on your shoulder.'

Knowing he was right, she mumbled, 'I'm sorry, I don't seem to be able to help it.'

'Well, if having famous parents bothers you that much, we'll keep quiet about it and pretend they don't exist…'

'It doesn't bother me, it's just—'

'Though, as I owe them a big debt of gratitude, I would have liked to invite them to the wedding.'

His hand had moved down to her breast and was playing with a pink nipple, sending little shafts of pleasure through her.

He had such power over her it was frightening.

Needing to assert herself a little, she said, 'I haven't said I'll marry you yet.'

'Well, I'm warning you, if you don't say yes, and name a date immediately, I'll make love to you until you do.'

'Mmm…' she murmured. Then, daringly, she added, 'It might be better to refuse then…'

He laughed joyously, and kissed her again. 'So long as I get the right answer in the end, I think I'll do things my way.'

CHAPTER FIVE

THE rest of the night was spent in a much more enjoyable occupation than talking, and they were having breakfast next morning in the penthouse's large sunny kitchen before Ryan once again brought up the subject of marriage.

'So when is the wedding to be?'

Virginia was perched on a stool opposite. Her face was shiny and innocent of make-up, her curly hair still damp from the shower.

She was wearing one of his white towelling bathrobes and it practically buried her, the shoulders halfway down her arms, the sleeves rolled up several times to leave her hands free.

He thought how lovely she was, how completely and utterly irresistible.

She looked up, her eyes, jade green in the bright sunshine, searching his face. 'Are you *certain* you want to marry me?'

'One hundred per cent.'

Watching her frown a little, as she returned to buttering her toast, he asked, 'You're not still having problems with the idea?'

'I keep wondering about your family. What if they object?'

'I'm certain they'll do nothing of the kind.'

'Just suppose they do?'

'As head of the family, I don't need their approval,' he pointed out evenly. 'But I'm sure they'll all be delighted for me. Beth in particular.'

'So to get back to my original question, when is it to be? And don't suggest spring. I don't want to wait that long.'

'When would you like it to be?'

'As soon as possible. The middle of December, say? That gives us about two months to plan everything.'

'Plan everything?' she echoed.

He raised an eyebrow at her. 'Why so surprised? Doesn't it usually take time to organise a wedding?'

'Not if it's a quiet one.'

'But ours isn't going to be a quiet one.'

'Oh, but—'

'If you were thinking of some hole in the corner affair, the answer's no. I want to flaunt my bride. I'd like us to get married at St Patrick's and have the kind of wedding that will take New York society by storm…'

Seeing he meant every word he said, she threw in the towel, and agreed dazedly. 'All right, if that's really what you want.'

'And if you have no objections, I'd still like to invite your parents.'

'Of course we'll invite them.'

'That's my girl.'

'I'm sorry to have been so stupid about the whole thing.'

Quietly, he suggested, 'I think your father should have the chance to give you away. Don't you?'

'I suppose so. Though I doubt if he'll want to.' Then realising how ungracious that sounded, she added, 'But we could always ask him.'

Ryan smiled at her and reached across the breakfast bar to take her hand and raise it to his lips.

'Now, with regard to the planning; I'm sure Beth will be only too happy to help… That is, if you'll let her?'

'Of course I'll let her… But are you sure she'll be all right? You said she'd had a heart attack.'

'I'm convinced that kind of excitement will only do her good.'

'In that case I'd be very grateful for her help.'

'Then, as soon as we're both dressed, we'll go down and give her the good news.'

To Virginia's relief, Beth, a romantic at heart, showed every sign of being as delighted as Ryan had forecasted, and if any of the others had any doubts, they kept them to themselves.

Her own parents, who lived in Soho in a handsome cast-iron building embellished with Italianate pillars and curlicues, were given the news the same morning.

Her mother, tall and dark-haired still, with the face of a dreamer, said she was pleased; while her father, grizzled and handsome, offered his congratulations and best wishes.

When Ryan suggested quietly that Brad might like to give his daughter away, to Virginia's surprise, he agreed at once. 'Just let me know the time and place.'

He produced a bottle of champagne and they toasted the engagement, before retreating back into their own little world.

After lunching in Chinatown, Ryan took Virginia to choose an engagement ring.

Dazzled by the vast selection of glittering stones, she finally picked out one that appealed to her.

'It's a sardonyx,' the jeweller explained, 'and a rare and beautiful one. The sardonyx is starting to gain popularity among the more romantically inclined because, in the language of gems, it means conjugal happiness.'

Liking its clear glowing amber colour, the antique setting, and most of all the sentiment attached to it, she glanced at Ryan, seeking his approval.

'Would you like to try it on?'

'Please.'

He slipped it on to her slender finger and, finding it a perfect fit, studied it for a moment before agreeing, 'Yes, it suits your hand.'

'You wouldn't sooner I had a diamond?'

Shaking his head, he said, 'Diamonds are a bit boring for you, my love.'

The endearment was all she needed to make her day perfect.

As though caught up in some magic spell, everything continued to go well. Janice was thrilled when they asked her to be bridesmaid, and accepted eagerly, while Steven declared himself delighted to act as best man.

Only Madeline, though staying coolly polite in front of Ryan, tended to make snide remarks when he wasn't around. Especially about Virginia's engagement ring.

'What exactly is it?' she enquired, looking down her nose at the large oval stone in its heavy gold setting.

'It's a sardonyx,' Virginia said quietly.

'How quaint. Wouldn't a diamond have been a better bet? It would be worth more if Ryan changed his mind and you got to keep it.'

But not even the older woman's spite could spoil Virginia's happiness, and she lived in a rainbow bubble of pure joy. Ryan loved her and they were going to be married; she would be part of a happy family. Her dream was coming true.

Though she spent a lot of her nights in his bed, concerned about what the family might think, she resisted all his urgings to move into the penthouse completely. She even refused to have a key.

When, after taking the first two weeks off to show her New York, Ryan reluctantly returned to work, Virginia, feeling the need to be independent, and unwilling to let him support her before they were married, decided it was time she did the same.

As they were lying in bed that night, pleasurably content after making love, she broached the subject. 'Ryan...'

'Mmm...?' Taking her hand, he separated her fingers, planting a kiss on each.

'I'd like to start my job at the gallery.'

'There's absolutely no need for you to work.'

'But I want to. If I don't, what shall I do with myself all day while you're at the office?'

'My love, there's your trousseau to buy and a wedding to organise... And, speaking of weddings, where would you like to go for our honeymoon?'

'I don't really mind.' Anywhere would be heaven with Ryan.

'Well, we could either find some snow and go skiing, or head for the sun. Do you have a preference?'

'Sun, I think.'

'Mexico? Hawaii? The Caribbean?'

'I've always wanted to go to Hawaii.'

'Then, Hawaii it is.' Gathering her close, he closed his eyes, thick dark lashes lying above his hard cheekbones like fans.

'Don't go to sleep yet,' she said.

He opened one eye. 'Does that mean you're not satisfied? You want more?'

'No, it means I've no intention of being sidetracked with all this talk of honeymoons.'

'Sidetracked? I don't know what you mean,' he said with a pretend innocence.

'You know perfectly well what I mean. I want to start the job you promised me.'

He groaned.

Tilting her face, she began to plant little baby kisses along his firm jaw line.

'Darling are you trying to cajole me?'

'Yes...'

'Well don't stop, I like it.'

'Ryan.'

'What about the wedding?'

'Beth, bless her heart, is doing most of the work, and seems to be having the time of her life.'

'Very well,' he capitulated with a sigh, 'if that's what

you really want. But do take a day off here and there to shop for your trousseau.'

'I will,' she agreed happily, and rewarded him with a kiss that eventually led to other things.

It was quite true that Beth was having the time of her life, and one day she said as much.

After a hectic and enjoyable morning of trousseau shopping, she and Virginia were eating lunch at Blundells and discussing the actual wedding day.

The ceremony had been scheduled for eleven o'clock, and afterwards there was to be a reception for two hundred guests at the Waldorf Astoria.

Her enthusiasm unabated, Beth said, 'I guess the next step will be to work out a seating plan.'

'Well as you know everyone and I don't, perhaps you'll advise me?'

'I'd be glad to.' Her cheeks a little flushed, the older woman admitted, 'I absolutely adore all the excitement of planning weddings. In fact there are times when I wish I was like Mrs Bennet and had five daughters to marry off.'

'Well, you're not far behind,' Virginia said with a smile. 'This is your second wedding and you still have another daughter to go…'

Shaking her head, Beth said, 'It's the first, actually. Madeline felt she wanted to do her own thing without any—'

She stopped speaking abruptly, but Virginia felt sure that the word on the tip of her tongue had been interference.

After a moment Beth went on almost apologetically, 'I know I should have asked sooner if you really minded me poking my nose in, but you were so nice about it that I…' The sentence tailed off.

'Of course I don't mind! And I've never thought of it as poking your nose in. In fact I don't know what I'd do without you.'

Looking relieved, Beth said, 'I did begin to wonder, as you have a mother of your own, if you would have preferred me to keep out of it.'

'Whatever put that idea into your head?' Virginia asked. Then realised that perhaps she should have asked, whoever?

Madeline, she was beginning to know, had an armoury of poisoned darts that she placed to do the most harm.

Giving Beth's hand an impulsive squeeze, she added, 'My own mother isn't the slightest bit interested, so it's lovely to have someone who is...'

As the older woman beamed her pleasure, Virginia added, 'Just promise me you won't overdo it.'

'If you mean my silly old heart, don't worry. Doing something I really enjoy is therapeutic.'

Her confidence fully restored, Beth went back to cheerfully discussing the seating arrangements for the reception.

'One of the first things we'll need to decide is who we put next to the ambassador. He's a charming man, and a good conversationalist...'

Though Virginia loved her job and enjoyed the days spent in the gallery, she always found herself eagerly anticipating the evenings spent in Ryan's company and the nights spent in his arms.

He was a wonderful lover, skilful and passionate, generous and tender, and the days and nights flew past in a whirl of happiness and excitement.

By the first week in December, most of the wedding arrangements had been made, leaving only a few things still to do.

Virginia was seeing less of Ryan now, as he worked late most evenings to tie in all the loose ends before their month in Hawaii.

On the Friday, Virginia took the day off and, accompanied by Beth, went to Claud Fucielle for the final fitting of her wedding gown.

Made of ivory silk, it was beautiful and romantic, with a medieval-type bodice and sleeves, and a full skirt that rustled when she moved.

As they drove back home after yet another afternoon of trousseau shopping, and tea and crumpets in the old-fashioned comfort of Myers, Beth queried, 'Will you be seeing Ryan this evening, or is he planning to work late again?'

'No, he isn't working, but I won't be seeing him. He mentioned having to attend a charity dinner.'

'Ryan's a good man. He gives to a lot of charities both here and abroad. In fact, though he rarely talks about it, he supports some of them practically single-handed...'

Yes, she could believe that, Virginia thought. Ryan was both caring and generous.

'Tell you what,' Beth pursued after a moment, 'if you've no other plans, why don't you have dinner with me? Janice is out, so I'll be on my own.'

The two had become firm friends, and Virginia answered at once, 'Thanks. I'd love to.'

Frowning a little, Beth added, 'I've just remembered that Steven's away on a business trip, so I suppose I ought to invite Madeline as well. Though I very much doubt if she'll want to come...

'Mrs Cluny usually serves dinner at seven-thirty. But don't wait till then, come down as soon as you're ready.'

When Virginia rang the bell at six-thirty, she felt nothing but relief to be told that Madeline had refused the invitation.

Echoing her thoughts, Beth went on, 'I must say I'm rather relieved that she had other plans. Somehow I don't find Madeline all that easy to be with.'

Neither of the women cared much for television so they spent a pleasant evening playing crib and listening to music, while they sprinkled a companionable silence with snippets of conversation, as people do when they're comfortable with each other.

It was almost eleven o'clock before they said their goodnights and Virginia left.

Wondering how late Ryan would be, she began to walk up to the next floor. She had just reached the top of the stairs when she saw that the penthouse door was open and two figures were standing in the doorway, very close together, and facing each other.

Ryan, his legs and feet bare, was wearing a short navy blue bathrobe, and Madeline, a black satin kimono with matching slippers. Her gleaming blonde hair hung round her shoulders.

She was very tall for a woman, and her pale head was almost on a level with his dark one. A long, scarlet-tipped hand resting on his sleeve, she was talking quietly, intimately.

Feeling awkward, Virginia hesitated.

Madeline cast the briefest glance her way; without seeming to notice her presence and, apparently wrapped up in each other, the pair kept talking.

A moment later Madeline put her arms around Ryan's neck and they kissed briefly but, to Virginia's eyes, passionately.

Suddenly chilled, she stood rooted to the spot while Madeline swept past, giving her a glittering glance that was at once inimical and triumphant.

'So where did you spring from?' Crossing the lobby to meet her, Ryan took Virginia's cold hand.

Through stiff lips, she said, 'I've been having dinner with Beth.' Even in her own ears her voice sounded strained and jerky.

Using the hand he was holding, he drew her into his arms and bent to kiss her mouth.

In a purely involuntary reaction, she turned her head away, so that his lips just brushed her cheek.

Straightening, he advised coolly, 'Don't let it throw you. It was just Madeline being...suppose we say...demonstrative...'

Demonstrative was the last thing Virginia would have suspected the ice-cool Madeline of being.

Seeing her troubled face, he tried to make light of it. 'Relatives do kiss you know.'

They were a close-knit family and relatives did kiss. But should sister-in-law and brother-in-law kiss in quite that way?

Drawing her towards the penthouse, he said, 'Come and tell me what kind of day you've had? How did the fitting go?'

As the door closed behind them, making an effort to match his casual tone, she said, 'Fine.'

When he would have gone straight through to the bedroom, she hung back, and with a faint sigh he led the way into the spacious living-room.

Remembering how Madeline had refused Beth's invitation, and wondering if they'd spent the evening together, she asked, 'What happened, did your dinner fall through?'

'No. It finished earlier than I'd expected.'

'Oh.'

'I got back about half an hour ago and rang your bell. When there was no answer, I presumed you were in the shower or something. If I'd realised you were with Beth I would have come down.'

Instead he'd apparently been having a tête-à-tête with Madeline... The thought came unbidden. She tried hard to dismiss it, and failed.

Watching her face, Ryan said briskly, 'Look, I think we'd better clear the air.'

Leading her to the couch, he gently pushed her down and took a seat beside her. 'I don't know what kind of scenario you're coming up with in that head of yours, but let me tell you straight away that Madeline and I had only been talking a couple of minutes. She didn't even come inside.

'I'd just finished taking a shower when I heard the bell. I went to the door fully expecting it to be you...'

While Virginia wanted desperately to believe him, a little demon of doubt pointed out that it was an odd time for a woman to call on her brother-in-law, dressed only in a kimono...

As though answering the thought, he explained, 'She'd popped up on the spur of the moment to ask me to choose between two possible wedding gifts, and to tell me how pleased she was for both of us...'

Reading Virginia's expression, he added, 'Yes, I must admit I took that with a pinch of salt. On the whole Madeline isn't the kind to be pleased for anyone but herself...

'However, I may be misjudging her, she certainly sounded genuine.'

'And that's when you kissed her?'

'I didn't kiss her. She kissed me.'

Then quizzically, he added, 'Now, have you finished giving me a hard time?'

'I'm sorry.' Her misgivings set completely at rest, she went into his arms like going home, and lifted her face for his kiss.

It was Janice who, a few evenings later, innocently put fresh doubts into Virginia's mind.

Not long in from the gallery, she was having a leisurely cup of tea in her kitchen, when the phone rang. She picked up the receiver to find it was her future sister-in-law, sounding excited.

'They've delivered my bridesmaid's dress, and a selection of headdresses. Mom's out, so can you spare a few minutes to come and help me choose which of them looks best.'

'I'll be straight down.'

Clad in her peach silk finery, Janice came flying to meet her. 'There's one or two that are out of this world! Come and take a look.'

The two women were in the midst of assessing the various headdresses when they were interrupted by the doorbell.

'That'll be Mom,' Janice said. Adding indulgently, 'She's always mislaying her key.'

'I'll go,' Virginia offered.

When she opened the door, her heart dropped to find it was Madeline, beautifully dressed as usual, her blonde chignon gleaming.

Brushing past without a word, she went through to the living-room, leaving the younger woman to follow.

'Where's Ryan? I'd like to talk to him.'

'I'm sorry, I'm afraid I don't know,' Virginia answered evenly.

'I felt sure he'd be with you. He's usually dancing attendance.'

The two younger women exchanged glances.

Surveying the expensive-looking bridesmaid dress and the collection of headdresses, Madeline observed, 'The amount this wedding must be costing, it's a blessing the family's a wealthy one.'

'Are you staying?' Janice asked shortly.

'No. Steven's taking me out to dinner. But I wanted a word with Ryan first.'

'Sorry we can't help you.' Janice sounded anything but sorry.

Moving towards the door, Madeline fired her parting shot. 'I presume poor Ryan didn't realise what he would be letting himself in for when he agreed to a big wedding.'

When the door had closed behind her, seeing the expression on Virginia's face, Janice advised sympathetically, 'Don't let her get to you.'

'I can't help it,' Virginia said unhappily. 'She makes me feel like a gold-digger.'

'Those cracks about the expense of a big wedding are rich coming from her. She was an aspiring actress who hadn't a cent to her name when she got her claws into Steven, and Mom spent a small fortune on their wedding without a word of thanks from her.

'She might be beautiful, but she's thirty-two, seven years older than Steven, and hard as nails. It's a great pity he ever married her. Ryan had more sense.'

'Ryan?'

Sounding a little awkward, Janice explained, 'Madeline was Ryan's lady friend first.'

Apparently realising that she'd said too much to stop there, she played it down. 'They had a brief fling before she transferred her attention to poor Steven.

'He's been besotted from the word go, a willing slave who worships the ground she walks on. How is it that men can be so blind? So easily dazzled by a beautiful face and figure?'

'Well so long as he's happy...' Virginia began hesitantly.

'I don't see how he *can* be happy,' Janice said gloomily. 'In the few months they've been married, she's made him jump through hoops and, since Ryan brought you back, I'll wager she hasn't been fit to live with.

'My guess is that when it was too late she realised she'd made a bad mistake: it was Ryan she really wanted. That's why she's so jealous of you. In fact, from the way she goes on, I get the impression she still thinks of Ryan as hers...

'But let's forget about her...' Selecting a band of small cream silk rosebuds, she set it on her smooth dark hair and asked, 'What do you think of this?'

The choice of headdresses finally narrowed down to two, so Beth could have a say, Virginia left Janice to it and made her way back to her own apartment.

All the time she had been smiling and attentive, part of

her mind had been trying to cope with the knowledge that Madeline and Ryan had been lovers before she had left him for Steven.

Sinking down onto the settee, staring blindly ahead, Virginia wondered what had made her leave him. While Steven was a lovely man, he hardly measured up as a serious rival to Ryan.

So perhaps Janice was right. Maybe, when it was too late, Madeline had realised that she'd made a bad mistake, and it was really Ryan she wanted.

Virginia went cold.

That kind of situation would almost certainly lead to tragedy, so she could only hope and pray that Janice was wrong.

But was she?

All at once Virginia's mind was filled with images of Madeline and Ryan kissing. If it was her own husband Madeline loved and wanted, would she have been kissing Ryan so passionately?

But even more important, knowing what had once been between them, why had Ryan allowed it to happen?

Or had he just allowed it. What if he'd lied when he'd said *she* had kissed *him*. What if the passion had been mutual?

No, Virginia told herself fiercely, a man like Ryan wouldn't carry on with his stepbrother's wife.

For one thing, if it came out it would destroy the family unity and break Beth's heart and, for another, he would be married himself in a few days' time.

He couldn't still want Madeline, or why would he have asked *her* to marry him? Though theirs had been a whirlwind romance, Ryan was hardly the kind of man to marry on the rebound.

* * *

Over the next few days Virginia did her best to push all the doubts and uncertainties away, but they returned time and again to haunt her.

She found herself thinking over every conversation she had had with Ryan, examining everything he had ever said or done.

He wanted her, she was sure of that... But did he *love* her? Though he had called her 'my love' from time to time, and had asked if she believed in love at first sight, he had never actually said the words, I love you.

And it might not even be *her* he wanted. Ryan was a red-blooded man, and if the woman he truly wanted was married to his stepbrother, perhaps any woman would have served the purpose?

Could she risk asking him how he really felt?

No, he would be bound to lie. He couldn't admit the truth and chance splitting the family.

But if he didn't love and want her, why had he chosen to marry her? She would have lived with him without any commitment, and he must have known that. So why had he decided to go the whole hog, to insist on a big society wedding that was sure to hit the headlines?

No, she must be what he wanted.

Still the doubts came creeping back, and Virginia began to sleep badly. Even when she was lying in Ryan's arms, she found herself unable to free her mind and rest.

Anxious to hide it, however, she made a gallant pretence of being her normal self. Which, judging by Ryan's sharp glances, failed to convince him.

When dark smudges like mauve bruises appeared beneath her eyes, he was driven to ask what was wrong.

'N-nothing,' she stammered.

Stroking her hair, he said, 'I'm quite certain there is. I'm beginning to know you, the way you have secret spaces, the way you keep part of yourself hidden, even from me...'

Then coaxingly, he asked, 'Why don't you tell me what's bothering you?'

When she remained silent, he persisted, 'Are you afraid I won't make a good husband?'

She shook her head.

'Scared I'll beat you, or keep you short of money?'

'Of course not.'

'Shall I go on with this guessing game, or are you going to tell me?'

Seeing he had no intention of giving up, she said desperately, 'Surely all brides-to-be have a few last-minute doubts?'

His indigo eyes studied her in a way that was both critical and assessing. 'Do they?'

Seizing the chance, she asked, 'Don't bridegrooms-to-be have any doubts?'

'In my case, none whatsoever,' he said firmly. 'I've never been so certain of anything in my life. I want you for my wife.'

Then, almost fiercely, he said, 'Don't let any doubts plague you. Just remember you're mine, and I'll never want to let you go.'

That night she slept, the sleep of sheer exhaustion, and got up the following morning feeling happier and more confident than she had felt since learning about Madeline and Ryan's 'fling'.

The next few days passed in a whirl of last-minute activity and, before she knew it, it was the eve of her wedding.

She and Ryan breakfasted together that morning and, before he left for his office, he kissed her and whispered huskily, 'I guess the next time I see you will be in St Pat's.'

Beth having said seriously that on their wedding day it was bad luck for Ryan to see his bride before they met in church, they had agreed to sleep apart that night.

Nor were they seeing each other in the evening. Steven had insisted on giving Ryan a stag party, while the women had a girls' night out at Martindales.

Martindales was a fun place with good food and an excellent floor show and, had there been only Beth and Janice, Virginia would have looked forward to it, but Madeline had announced her intention of coming. Which made a difference.

In the event it proved to be a great deal more pleasant than Virginia had anticipated. Not only did Madeline keep her claws sheathed, but she actually went out of her way to be agreeable.

The champagne flowed freely and, by the time the night was over and they reached Falconer's Tower, they were somewhat merry.

When the elevator had carried them upwards, they all got out in the lower foyer and stood for a moment or two talking before they said their goodnights.

As Madeline let herself into her own apartment, Beth said to Virginia, 'Have a good night's sleep, and give us a call in the morning when you're ready for some help getting dressed.'

'Thanks, I will.'

'I'm so pleased you're going to be part of the family.'

'So am I,' Janice added warmly.

The three women exchanged hugs and, as mother and daughter bickered gently over who had the key, Virginia made her way upstairs.

Her dream of being part of a happy family would soon be true, and she walked on air.

She had been in her apartment only long enough to take off her coat, when the doorbell rang.

It was a few minutes before twelve and, hoping it was Ryan calling in to say goodnight, she hurried to open it.

To her surprise, it was Madeline.

Without waiting for an invitation, the blonde walked in. 'I came to tell you how happy I am about the wedding, and bring you this. It will do for something borrowed.'

Opening the small flat box, Virginia found a pretty satin and lace garter.

'Why, thank you, it's lovely. I'll be sure to let you have it back.'

Madeline's beautiful teeth gleamed in a smile. 'Don't worry, I always get back what's mine.'

Puzzled by the other's tone, but deciding to ignore it, Virginia said, 'And I'm glad you're happy about the wedding.'

'Though I knew Ryan was doing it for *us*, I must confess that there have been times when I've felt a little jealous.'

'I don't understand,' Virginia said blankly.

'You mean he didn't tell you why he was marrying you? But perhaps he thought it was best not to. After all, ignorance is bliss, so they say.'

In a voice she scarcely recognised as her own, Virginia said, 'I think I'd sooner know.'

'Well, you see, Ryan and I were lovers before I married Steven—'

'I'm aware of that.'

Just for an instant Madeline looked put out, then she went on, 'We had a red-hot affair, but when passions run high so do tempers.

'He'd been hedging about getting married, and we quarrelled. I started to go out with Steven. I only did it to bring Ryan to heel but, though he's always been mad about me, he can be stubborn.

'I'd learnt my lesson, so I refused to sleep with Steven. When he got desperate enough to propose, I decided I'd be a fool not to accept—'

Breaking off, Madeline said sharply, 'There's no need to look so disgusted. If you're thinking I'm a gold-digger, well, it takes one to know one... And after all, a girl has to look after herself...

'Though I must admit that as soon as we were married,

I regretted it. I knew I'd made a bad mistake, that I'd never got over Ryan...'

So Janice had been right, after all.

'One night when Steven was out, Ryan and I kissed, and all the old passion flared up. We became lovers again, meeting whenever we could, sometimes here, sometimes in town...

'But after a while, Ryan called a halt in case anyone was getting suspicious. He was very concerned about upsetting Beth and the family, or causing a public scandal...'

Her voice as cold as her heart, Virginia asked, 'So what have I to do with it?'

'Ryan decided that if he was safely and publicly married, with all the trimmings and the bride's parents in attendance, it would avoid the risk of any scandal and paint a picture of good, solid respectability.

'In other words, it should make a perfect smokescreen. So long as we're discreet, who's going to suspect a newly married man of playing around with his sister-in-law? No one. Least of all his loving family...'

Virginia felt as if she'd been kicked in the stomach. It was so perfectly logical. It made sense of all the things that had puzzled her: why Ryan had swept her off her feet in the first place; why he'd rushed her into agreeing to marry him; why he had been so keen to tell the family; why he'd opted for a big wedding; why he had never actually said he loved her...

'Which means that we'll all be happy...' Madeline's smile held an almost feline satisfaction.

Her voice hoarse, Virginia exclaimed, 'If you think for one instant that I'll go along with it, you're mad...!'

'I don't see what you've got to lose. You'll still have everything you're marrying him for: jewels, clothes, a wonderful lifestyle, anything that money can buy... And let's face it, Ryan's man enough to keep the both of us happy.'

'Get out!' Virginia cried. 'Take this and get out!' Thrusting the garter into Madeline's hand, she opened the door.

'Suit yourself,' Madeline said. 'But when you've had a chance to think about it, you'll see I'm right.'

Her head feeling as if an iron band was tightening round it, her stomach heaving, Virginia leaned against the closed door.

When the nausea subsided a little, in a voice she didn't recognise as her own, she called a taxi and, her whole being clenched into a knot of anguish, went through to the bedroom to pack.

Ignoring the bags already packed for her honeymoon, she gathered together just the things she had brought with her, and bundled them into her old suitcases.

Then leaving her engagement ring and everything that Ryan had paid for, taking only the money she had earned, dry-eyed and frozen inside, she closed the apartment door behind her and rode the elevator down.

Her dream was over.

As luck would have it, the security booth was empty, the night-security guard out doing his rounds.

Hurrying across the lobby, she put down her cases while she released the dead-bolt. A moment later she had slipped out without being seen and, her cases banging against her legs, was hurrying towards the waiting yellow cab.

Her luggage stowed, the driver asked, 'Where to, lady?'

'The airport, please.'

'JFK?'

'Yes.'

CHAPTER SIX

SHIVERING, feeling all the despair and desolation she had felt at that moment, Virginia came back to the present.

After a moment, his fair face still showing his concern, Charles asked, 'So what did you do then?'

'I sat in the airport until morning, then I managed to get a seat on an early flight to Heathrow. By the time I should have been getting married, I was more than halfway back to England.

'When I got to London I booked in at a cheap hotel, and on Monday morning I started looking for a job... The rest you know.'

Frowning, Charles remarked, 'You haven't mentioned leaving a note or anything.'

'I didn't.'

'You mean you left without a word to anyone?'

'Yes... I suppose I was in a state of shock. I certainly wasn't in any condition to think straight. And what could I have said? What possible reason could I have given for not going through with the wedding? The truth would have torn the family apart, and Beth had a weak heart...'

'You didn't consider tackling Falconer?'

She shook her head. 'I couldn't bear the humiliation. I never wanted to see him again.'

'I take it you continued to feel that way?'

'Yes. That was why I didn't want my parents to know where I was. They might have told him.'

'I see. So you were virtually in hiding, and that's why you'd dropped the Adams, and were calling yourself Virginia Ashley?'

'Yes.' Despairingly, she added, 'I was just beginning to feel safe. It was an awful shock to see him in the gallery.'

Charles squeezed her sympathetically. 'I could tell his presence affected you deeply. In fact I wondered at the time if you were in love with him?'

'I just don't know,' she said, and tried to tell herself it was the truth.

'Taking everything into consideration,' Charles remarked seriously, 'it's just as well Falconer didn't see you.'

She bit her lip. 'I'm afraid he did.'

'How do you know?' he asked sharply.

'I walked home through the park. He'd been waiting in the mews, and he followed me.'

Charles's mouth tightened. 'Did he speak to you?'

'Yes.'

'He didn't touch you, did he? I'll break his damn neck if he did.'

That kind of wild threat was so unlike Charles's usual pragmatic approach that, scared of what might happen if he took on Ryan, she stammered, 'N-no...not really. I mean, he just put his hands over my eyes and said, "Guess who?"'

'But he scared you?'

'Yes, he scared me. He said...' Her voice shook so much she had to stop and take a steadying breath before she could go on. 'He said he wants me back.'

Charles stiffened. 'Wants you back? After the shabby way he treated you! Why does he want you back?'

'He was furious at the way I'd left him and spoilt all his plans. He said there was a score to settle.'

She folded her arms over her chest, rubbing them as if she were cold. 'I told him I had absolutely no intention of ever going back to him.'

'Falconer doesn't look to me like the kind of man who would take no for an answer.'

'He isn't.' She swallowed hard, then said in a rush,

'That's why I told him we were living together. I hope you don't mind?'

'No, of course I don't mind.' With dry humour, he added, 'Taken one way, it's true. Taken the other, it's flattering.'

After a moment he asked carefully, 'Was that what finally got rid of him?'

'Not exactly...'

'So how did you shake him off?'

'A little boy who was playing with a toy yacht fell in the lake, and while Ryan was pulling him out I made myself scarce and took a taxi home.'

Then, urgently, she said, 'Charles, I don't want to go back to him.'

'I'm very glad to hear it.' He patted her hand. 'There's no need to look so fraught; he can't force you to.'

'No, that's what I keep telling myself.'

After a thoughtful silence, he remarked, 'I presume it was seeing Falconer again that made you change your mind about marrying me?'

'Yes,' she said in a small voice.

'Then I suppose I should be grateful that fate brought him into the gallery, and gave you a chance to realise you no longer loved him...'

Though Virginia felt a strong sense of shame, she let it go.

'Now you've got your feelings sorted out once and for all,' Charles went on, 'you'll be able to put him right out of your mind... And, before too long, he'll be safely back in the States.'

Agitated and guilty because she hadn't told Charles the whole truth by a long chalk, she bit her lip.

His eyes on her face, he said quietly, 'Something's still bothering you. Would you like to tell me what it is?'

'What am I going to do until he *does* go back?' she burst out. 'He could walk into the gallery any time.'

'I'll tell you what you can do, you can take a few days off...'

'Oh but—'

'No buts. Helen and I can manage for a while and, if he does happen to come in, I'll deal with him.'

Seeing the look of doubt on her face, he asked, 'What's wrong? Don't you think I'm capable of dealing with a man like Falconer?'

'I'm sure you are,' she said with a great deal more confidence than she felt. 'And I'm equally sure that, instead of letting things get out of hand, you can do it diplomatically.'

'Then, what's the problem?'

There were more problems than she could shake a stick at. Remembering Ryan's mocking, 'Be seeing you,' she shivered.

But if she stayed in the house and refused to open the door to him, she'd be safe enough. He could hardly break in.

Seeing Charles was waiting for an answer, she managed a smile. 'Maybe I'm just being paranoid.'

'I'm convinced you are, so stop worrying.'

'I'll try,' she promised.

'Now let's forget all about Falconer and get back to a much more pleasant subject. You said you'd be happy with a quiet wedding.'

'Yes.'

'Would you like to be married in church, or at the register office?'

'Church, I think. If that's all right with you?'

He smiled and gave her a little squeeze. 'I'd prefer to be married in church myself. First thing in the morning I'll have a talk with the Reverend Peter Coe, the vicar of St Giles—he's a personal friend of mine—and see how soon it can be arranged. It can't be soon enough for me.' His arms tightening, he added deeply, 'I'll do my utmost to make you happy.'

When he tilted her face and began to kiss her, she willed herself to relax and enjoy it.

After a while his kisses grew more ardent, and she had to quell a little twist of anxiety. What would she do if he wanted to take her to bed?

Throughout her stay in his house, Charles had behaved like a perfect gentleman. But he was a man, after all, a man she had just promised to marry. And now she had told him about her relationship with Ryan, he must feel he had a right to the same privileges.

She had no doubt that he would be a caring and sensitive lover, and once she had made a commitment it would set the seal on their future together. It might even help to drive Ryan from her mind.

But when, his fair face a little flushed, Charles took her hand and began to lead her up the stairs, her steps were oddly reluctant.

Feeling that reluctance, he paused on the landing, his eyes on her face, puzzled, a little pleading. Gritting her teeth, knowing it wouldn't be fair to him to back out now, she turned and led the way into her bedroom.

Drawing her close, his ardour returning, he began to kiss her once more and, putting her arms around his neck, she forced herself to respond.

He was passionate yet tender, the kind of man almost any woman would be pleased to have as a lover, and closing her eyes she tried to concentrate on enjoying his kisses.

His lips brushed the side of her neck and slid to the smoothness of her shoulder. 'You're so beautiful,' he murmured, 'so soft and warm and truly feminine. I've never known a woman who affected me as much as you do.'

She was very conscious of his touch, of every move he was making. Too conscious. If only she could lose herself in the warmth of his lovemaking. Instead, her mind seemed to stand apart, a cool spectator, treating the experience like some ordeal that must be endured, rather than enjoyed.

Suddenly he let her go and drew back, his face impatient, baffled. 'What's wrong, Virginia?'

'N-nothing,' she stammered.

'Something must be. It's like trying to make love to the Venus de Milo.'

'I'm sorry, truly I am.' She sought for an excuse. 'It's been such a traumatic day that I...I just...' Her grey-green eyes filled with tears.

His face softened at once. 'I'm an insensitive brute. I should have realised you'd still be upset. Forgive me.'

Desperately ashamed of the way she was treating him, especially as he was being so sweet about it, but quite unable to remedy matters, she found herself repeating helplessly, 'I'm sorry.'

'It's all right, really it is. I shouldn't have rushed you.' He kissed her forehead. 'Now, off you go to bed, and don't worry about a thing.'

At the door he turned to add, 'Once Falconer's gone back and we're married, it will all come right, I promise you.'

The following morning they ate breakfast together as usual, before Charles prepared to set off for the gallery at his normal time, but alone.

Her actions unconsciously wifely, Virginia accompanied him into the hall.

At the door he kissed her cheek gently, and said, 'You know where I am if you want me for anything.'

Her beautiful eyes reflecting how lost she suddenly felt, she said uncertainly, 'I'm not sure what I'll find to do all day.'

'Why not go into town?'

No, she dared not do that; Ryan might be having her watched.

Well aware that Charles was concerned about her, she said more cheerfully, 'Perhaps I'll just do a spot of spring-cleaning.'

'Isn't it a bit late for spring-cleaning? In any case that's the kind of thing I pay Mrs Crabtree for.

'Come on, you haven't had a break since you started at the gallery, so make the best of it, just relax and catch up on some reading... Pretend you're on holiday. If it keeps fine and hot, as it's forecast to, you could make some sangria and sit outside and get tanned.'

At the rear of the house there was a green and pleasant garden that caught the morning and early afternoon sun. It boasted a small paved area, and some comfortable patio furniture.

'How lovely and decadent!' Her spirits lifting a little, she added, 'I might just do that.'

Then only too grateful for his unstinting kindness and caring, she said, 'Tell you what else I'll do, I'll cook you a really nice meal for tonight.'

'Wonderful!' Grinning at her boyishly, he added, 'A man who's hoping to do business with me has insisted on taking me out to lunch, but I'll be sure to have something light.

'Oh, just one thing, can you time dinner for a bit later than usual?'

'Seven-thirty?'

'To be on the safe side, make it eight.'

Her heart sank. 'Fine.'

Knowing it wasn't fine at all, he explained, 'After the gallery's closed, I have a business appointment. A very important one, otherwise I would have cancelled it.'

With unusual animation, he added, 'If all goes well, it should mean a virtual end to my financial problems.'

'Oh, that's marvellous.'

'I'll give you all the details later... Don't worry about a thing, now.' He kissed her, and was gone.

Standing staring at the closed door, she felt a sense of loss. The whole day stretched ahead, flat and empty, with nothing to do but think of Ryan...

Tuesday was one of the days Mrs Crabtree didn't come

in, so Virginia spent the first part of the morning washing the breakfast dishes and doing a spot of housework.

She was just about to look in the freezer, when the phone rang.

This might be him.

No, she really was getting paranoid. Ryan would believe her to be at the gallery. In fact the only person who would expect anyone to be home at this time of day would be Charles.

Going through to the hall she picked up the receiver and said, 'Hello?'

'Not sunbathing yet?'

As she had surmised, it was Charles.

'No, not yet.'

Sounding unusually animated, he went on, 'I've had a talk with Peter and he's suggested going for a special licence. That way we can get married in a few days' time.'

A few days' time.

Rather than being a promise that could be fulfilled at some unspecified future date, it was suddenly on top of her, breathing down her neck.

'Because it's June, and June is the month for weddings apparently, the church is fully booked on Saturday, but we could be married on Monday, if you're in agreement?'

Monday was less than a week away.

Though Virginia was still sure she was doing the right thing, just for a split second, the thought of their wedding being quite so soon threw her.

After a barely perceptible hesitation, she said, 'Yes...'

He picked up that hesitation. 'You don't sound too certain?'

Virginia took a deep breath. 'Yes, I'm quite certain. Monday will be great.'

She heard his sigh of relief.

'The next thing we'll need to discuss is a honeymoon. In the meantime, be thinking where you'd like to go.'

'What about the gallery?'

'If I can't get someone in to help Helen, I'll close it. The start of our married life is much more important than the gallery...'

How could she go wrong with a husband like that? she thought, her heart swelling.

'I'm getting another call coming through, so I'd better go. I'll try not to be too late tonight...'

When they had said their goodbyes, she replaced the receiver and went back to the kitchen to take the chicken portions for their evening meal out of the freezer.

That done, she sliced fresh lemons to make lemonade, before changing her jeans and shirt for old denim shorts and a tank top, and taking her long curly hair up in a ponytail.

Then, having poured herself a glass of lemonade from the covered jug, she picked up a new book she hadn't yet found time to read, and barefoot, carried them both outside into the sunshine.

The garden was high-walled and private, surrounded by neighbouring gardens, so that the only way into it was through the house. She would be quite safe here.

Although the book seemed to be well-written and the story showed every sign of being an exciting one, she was unable to concentrate. Ryan's dark face kept coming between her and the printed page, and she found herself wondering anxiously what his next move would be...

'Good morning. Sleep well?'

As though her thoughts had conjured him up, there he was, lounging in the kitchen doorway, dressed in well-cut trousers and a white silk shirt open at the neck.

The shock was so great that she jumped to her feet, dropping the glass she was holding. It smashed to smithereens on the paving stones, splashing her with sticky lemonade.

He clicked his tongue. 'Dear me, how very careless.

Don't move your feet in case you tread on some broken glass.'

His warning came too late. She gave a little cry as a sharp sliver jabbed into her big toe.

'Sit down, let me take a look.' He pushed her gently back into her seat. Then, crouching on his haunches he lifted her slim foot and eased out the needle-sharp piece of glass.

A spot of bright-red blood welled.

Bending his dark head he put his mouth to the wound and sucked, causing a kick of desire that made her stomach clench and her mouth go dry.

Then, having run his tongue tip over the broken skin to feel for any tiny particles of glass that might have remained, he said cheerfully, 'That's fine.'

Still holding her foot and looking up at her through lashes any female might have envied, he added quizzically, 'You're the only woman I've ever known who has feet beautiful enough to start a foot fetish. Now, stay where you are, otherwise I might have to do that all over again.'

Disappearing into the kitchen, he returned after a moment with a plastic dustpan and brush and swept up the scattered pieces of glass with neat efficiency.

'I see there's more lemonade in the jug, so as soon as I've disposed of the debris I'll pour some for us both, and join you.'

Virginia was still trying to pull herself together when he returned with two glasses and, putting them on the low table, dropped into the lounger alongside her own, handsome as Lucifer and twice as dangerous.

With cool insolence he let his eyes travel slowly over her from head to toe, making her very conscious of her bare legs.

Studying the denim shorts, the tank top, and the ponytail, he mocked, 'Dressed like that you look for all the world like a fifteen-year-old schoolgirl.'

Finding her voice, she said thickly, 'But I'm not. I'm almost twenty-five.'

'Which is just as well. The word I left out of my description was desirable.'

Alarmed by the little flame burning in his eyes, she demanded, 'What are you doing here? What do you want?' Then, in confusion, she asked, 'How did you get in?'

Smiling at her consternation, he answered, 'Through the front door, like any respectable visitor.'

'You would have needed a key.'

'I have one.' With an air of satisfaction, he displayed a key, before slipping it back into his pocket.

'Where did you get that?' she asked sharply.

Unblushingly, he admitted, 'I borrowed it from your purse last night.'

Too late she recalled how the purse she had dropped had been picked up and placed on the hall table, where it still lay.

Seeing the impotent anger in eyes now darkened to the colour of charcoal, he added, 'I was rather hoping you wouldn't miss it. In any operation, the element of surprise is a valuable one, and I've always found it pays to wrong-foot your opponent.'

'Do you have to sound so damn smug?' she burst out furiously.

He shook his head reprovingly. 'Temper.'

Realising that if she kept rising to the bait she was playing right into his hands, she struggled to regain some composure.

When she could trust her voice, she said, 'I don't know what you hope to gain by this. I've no intention of coming back to you.'

'So you said,' he agreed. 'That's one of the reasons I'm here, to try and change your mind.'

'How did you know I'd be at home?'

'First thing this morning I called in at the gallery and had a word with Raynor.'

Her blood ran cold.

'I have to admit I was mistaken about him. He's no wimp.' Ryan sounded as if he was relishing the thought of some stout opposition. 'Though he looks ineffectual, he stood up to me with the kind of backbone I was forced to admire…'

Seeing the look of horror on her face, he smiled with wry amusement. 'To set your mind at rest, I meant verbally, rather than physically…'

She breathed a sigh of relief.

But standing up to Ryan, even when the conflict was verbal, was no mean feat. She knew quite well how, without ever raising his voice, he could intimidate all but the strongest of men.

'So you won't need to bind his wounds.'

Ignoring the sarcasm, she demanded anxiously, 'What did you say to him?'

'Considerably less than he said to me.' His voice as brittle as ice, Ryan added, 'It was most interesting and instructive.'

Holding her breath, Virginia waited.

After a moment, Ryan went on, 'Then he called me a swine, and told me straight that if he ever did manage to locate and buy *Wednesday's Child*, he had no intention of letting me have it, so there was no further need to come into the gallery.'

'Is that all?'

'No. According to him, I've upset you enough. I gather the only occasion he actually knows about is our dalliance in the park.'

'Hardly a dalliance,' she said resentfully.

Ignoring the interruption, Ryan continued, 'If he'd been aware that I knew where you were living, and had been to the house last night, he would never have left you at home by yourself...' Then, like a whiplash, he asked, 'Why didn't you tell him about my visit?'

'I—I didn't want to upset him.'

'He'd be a great deal more upset if he knew I was here now,' Ryan observed with satisfaction.

Trying to keep some kind of grip on the situation, she asked, 'Why are you here? Apart from trying to change my mind.'

His blue-violet eyes narrowed against the sun and, gleamed through thick dark lashes as he explained idly, 'I thought I'd take you out to lunch.'

'Then think again! I've no intention of having lunch with you.'

Unruffled, he agreed, 'Just as you like. We don't *have* to go out to lunch. And, on second thoughts, you're quite right. It will be a lot more fun to stay here.'

Virginia bit her lip, recognising belatedly that it would have been much safer to lunch in some public place, rather than be here alone with him.

Her apprehension was compounded when he added, 'It will give us plenty of time to...shall we say...indulge other appetites?'

'No!' Agitation brought her to her feet. 'I'm going to marry Charles. If you lay so much as a finger on me I'll...I'll...'

'You'll what?'

He took a step towards her. She retreated until the wall of the house brought her up short.

Following her, he put a hand each side of her head, flat-palmed against the stucco, trapping her there.

'Tell me, Virginia, did you dream of me after I'd gone last night?'

'No, I didn't.' She spat the words at him. 'I told you there'd be no need to.'

His face grew taut. 'You didn't sleep with Raynor?' he asked sharply.

She wanted to say she had to get back at him but, remembering the uncomfortable little scene in her bedroom, how she'd treated Charles, somehow she couldn't...

A hand beneath her chin, Ryan lifted her face to scrutinise it. 'Did you?'

'Whether I did or not is nothing to do with you.'

She heard the breath hiss through his teeth before he said, 'From now on I'm going to be the only man who makes love to you. I've been waiting so long to...' Putting his lips to her ear, he whispered graphic details of all the things he'd been waiting to do to her.

The erotic images his words provoked made her stomach fold in on itself and a shiver run through her. As she struggled to appear unmoved, she heard his soft chuckle.

'You respond so beautifully, my pet. Your body is already reacting to the mere thought of being made love to...'

It was true. Her nipples had grown firm and were plainly visible through the thin material of her close-fitting tank top.

'And that's such a turn on...'

He traced them with a fingertip, making pleasure tingle through her, before querying softly, 'So which is it to be? Shall we go to bed and see how long you can hold out? Or would you like to have lunch with me after all?'

'Yes,' she said desperately.

With a slightly crooked smile, he asked, 'Which?'

Her voice hoarse and impeded, she said, 'I'd like to have lunch with you.'

'Good. Somehow I thought you'd come round to my way of thinking.'

Holding her upper arms, he kissed her lightly. 'Though I must admit it might have been more flattering, and a great deal more fun, if you'd decided to go to bed. Still, I can wait. I've already waited for well over two years, so a few more days aren't going to make that much difference.

'Now suppose you go and put on something a shade

more suitable for lunching at Moonrakers. I'll give you fifteen minutes.'

He released her and sat down again.

Marvelling at what lengths he would go to to get what he wanted, she fled into the house and up the stairs.

When she reached her room, her first thought was to barricade herself in, but almost immediately she realised how impractical that idea was. Reluctantly abandoning the idea and afraid that he might come looking for her if she exceeded the fifteen minutes he'd allowed, she showered and dried herself quickly.

Then coiling her hair into a neat chignon, she donned fresh undies and the grey silk suit she usually wore to work. A touch of make-up to boost her morale, and the glasses to hide behind, she was once more a businesswoman rather than the fifteen-year-old schoolgirl he'd called her.

She even had a few minutes to spare.

If she gathered up her purse and went quietly out of the front door, once at the end of the street, she would have a good chance of picking up a cruising taxi before he even realised she was gone.

Holding her breath, she crept down the stairs carefully avoiding the tread that she knew squeaked and, crossing the hall, reached for her purse.

It was no longer there.

Well, she would ask the taxi driver to take her to the gallery, and borrow the fare from Charles, even if it meant telling him the whole truth.

Her hand was on the latch when Ryan's mocking voice asked, 'Trying to sneak off without me?'

She jumped a mile, and spun round to find his big frame filling the living-room doorway.

'It's just as well I was on my guard.'

'Damn you!' she muttered helplessly.

Strolling over, he stood looking down at her suit, the heavy glasses, and the neat coil of hair.

An unholy gleam in his eye, he murmured, 'My, my...how very restrained and businesslike.'

'You said "something a shade more suitable."'

'The only place a get-up like that is suitable for is a place of work. However it can be remedied to some extent... When did you start wearing these awful glasses?'

'Some time ago,' she answered stiffly. 'And I don't think they're awful.'

He lifted the despised glasses off her nose and squinted through them. 'You don't need these, they're plain glass.' Tossing them carelessly onto the hall table, he added, 'It's much too late for disguises.'

Then, before she could protest, his deft fingers were plucking out the pins that held her chignon in place.

'That's a lot better,' he said triumphantly, as her ash-brown hair tumbled around her shoulders. 'Now at least I won't look as if I'm having lunch with some school-marm.'

'Go to hell!' she burst out.

With a plaintive sigh, he protested, 'Now, is that kind?' Then, coaxingly, he said, 'I think, having hurt my feelings, you should kiss me better.'

His eyes crossed, he pursed his lips in readiness.

Caught unawares, she almost laughed. He'd always been totally irresistible when he was clowning.

'Go on,' he urged, 'quickly, because Maxwell and the limousine are waiting outside.'

'I've no intention of kissing you.' But she was seriously tempted, and her voice shook betrayingly.

'Then I'll kiss you.'

'I don't want you to kiss me.'

'Of course you want me to kiss you. You just don't want to admit it.'

A second later his mouth was covering hers. He wasn't holding her, and she could have moved away. Instead she stood as though she was glued to the spot while his lips teased hers, coaxing them to part for him.

When they did, his arms closed around her and he deepened the kiss until her head reeled and nothing in the world existed but Ryan.

She was dimly aware of his heart thudding—or was it her own?—the rapid rise and fall of his chest, and the masculine scent of his aftershave.

Beneath her palms his silk shirt felt cool and fresh, until the heat of his body seeped through...

When he finally released her, he was breathing like a man who had just lost a race, and she was totally dazed, mindless. His for the taking.

If he had just led her upstairs she would have gone, but instead, his voice ragged, he gave her a chance to back out. 'Would you like to change your mind about going out to lunch?'

Somehow, she made herself answer, 'No, I wouldn't.'

'Hoist with my own petard,' he commented ruefully.

But she sensed it was what he'd wanted her to say, as though going out to lunch was part of some bigger, more important plan.

CHAPTER SEVEN

OPENING the door, he escorted her down the steps to where a limousine was waiting by the kerb. The chauffeur, who was lounging in the sun, straightened up at their approach and held open the door.

When Ryan had helped her in, he slid in beside her and picked up a jacket that had been lying on the seat. Taking a tie from the pocket, he put it around his neck and knotted it, remarking ironically, 'Must observe the niceties.'

By the time they reached their destination, a pleasant top-floor restaurant only about half a mile from the gallery, and close to Kenelm Park, Virginia had recovered enough to appear at least outwardly composed.

Though at first glance Moonrakers appeared to be full, and the one unoccupied table near the door bore a reserved notice, Ryan was greeted by name, and a table for two was immediately set up in a secluded corner.

'Don't tell me,' she said tartly, 'you have a stake in the place.'

Once again she felt the almost overwhelming pull of his attraction as, grinning, he denied it. 'Not this time, I'm afraid. The owner happens to be a friend of mine.'

'How fortunate.'

'Isn't it?' His eyes were warm and teasing.

Feeling her spirits lift, she was halfway to enjoying herself when, abruptly recalling the past and what he was trying to do, she was shaken by how close she had been to liking him again.

While they ordered and the meal was served, Ryan made an effort to keep up a light, entertaining conversation.

But retiring into her defensive shell, refusing to come

out and play his game, she answered in monosyllables when she was forced to answer at all.

At length he enquired, 'Something wrong?'

'What could possibly be wrong?' she asked sarcastically.

'You seemed to be opening up a little and then suddenly, snap, you're oyster-tight again! Why don't you make an effort to relax, so we can enjoy our lunch together?'

'You might have coerced me into having lunch with you, but it doesn't mean I have to enjoy it.'

With a slight shrug, he let it go and lapsed into silence. But she was conscious that he watched her constantly, as if he was unable to keep his eyes off her.

The food was good but she ate automatically, tasting very little, her mind beset by uneasy questions.

After that searching and passionate kiss in the hallway, he must have known she was his for the taking, so why had he offered her a chance to back out?

She could only be thankful that he had, but the question remained, why? Why had he been so determined to take her out to lunch? Ryan wasn't the kind of man to do anything without a good reason...

She was still pondering that unanswerable why, as they drank their coffee.

'When did you agree to marry Raynor?' Ryan's smooth, casual-sounding query came out of the blue.

Her head came up sharply. 'What?'

'I asked when you agreed to marry Raynor?'

She braced herself. 'Charles told you we were getting married?'

'He told me you were *planning* to.'

Remembering how Ryan had said, 'Over my dead body', she blenched. 'Y-you didn't...?'

'Beat him up? No of course I didn't. I merely warned him what the consequences would be if he didn't back off, and smartly.'

She put a hand to her mouth.

'What did you expect me to do, *congratulate* him?'

When she said nothing, he persisted smoothly, 'So tell me, Virginia, when did you accept Raynor's proposal?'

Ryan never missed a trick, she thought with some bitterness.

Carefully, she said, 'It's a few weeks since he asked me to marry him.'

'And did you say yes straight away?'

'Of course I did. I love him.'

'If I remember rightly, you said, "Passionately."'

'Yes... Passionately.'

Ryan sucked in his breath, and his eyes wickedly amused, charged, 'The lies fairly hop out of you.'

'I told you in the park that Charles and I were going to be married.'

'No you didn't. You said, "He wants to marry me," which is quite a different kettle of fish. Why don't you be honest and admit that when he first asked you you turned him down. You only agreed to marry him after what happened last night.'

'I did no such thing,' she denied stoutly.

'Don't bother with any more lies. Raynor admitted it was only last night that you agreed. Which tells me a great deal... Though he put a somewhat different interpretation on it. You see he's under the impression that you agreed to marry him when you discovered you were finally over me. Would he be quite so happy if he realised that you're only using him as a kind of safeguard?'

'No, it's not like that. I'm very fond of Charles, and I respect him. He'll make a good husband and father.'

'So you've discussed having a family?'

'Yes.'

'How many children did you decide on?'

Though well aware that he was deriding her, she answered, 'Four.'

'So you accepted his proposal, made plans to have children, but you still didn't sleep with him.'

'Did he tell you that too?'

'He didn't need to. Apart from a couple of remarks he made that were dead giveaways, I know a frustrated man when I see one. And he's absolutely mad about you. He may soon start putting you under pressure.'

'As you've done?' she flashed.

'Ah, but there's a difference.'

'A difference?'

'You want to sleep with me,' he said softly. 'You don't want to sleep with him.'

'What makes you so sure?'

'If you had wanted to sleep with Raynor you would have done it before now.'

'I've already told you—'

'Indeed you have, so don't bother telling me yet again how good a lover he is, and how he's not hidebound enough to simply take you to bed. I don't believe you've been sleeping with him. Otherwise you would have done so last night.'

Rattled because he was whang in the gold, she mocked, 'When did you become a psychologist?'

'It doesn't take a psychologist to work that one out, any more than it takes a mathematician to add two and two.'

'What kind of expert would it take to work out that you're wasting your time? That it really doesn't matter whether or not I've already slept with Charles—'

'You know it matters to me. Some children will happily share the same lollipop, but even as a young child I always wanted one that was mine alone.'

Ignoring the interruption, she ploughed on, 'What *does* matter is that I'm going to marry him, and that I'm not coming back to you.'

'That's where you're wrong,' he said with quiet certainty. 'But we'll talk about it later.'

After a glance at his watch, he signalled the waiter and paid the bill. Then, an arm around her waist, he began to lead her towards the door.

Head down, she was trying to think how best to get away from him when he paused and, an odd note in his voice, said softly, 'Virginia...'

As she glanced up, he bent and kissed her full on the lips, and lingeringly.

Ryan wasn't a man to be demonstrative in such a public place and, taken completely by surprise, she stood motionless until he lifted his head and began to walk once more.

Caught up in the circle of his arm, she moved as a sleepwalker might, until the sight of a fair-haired man staring at her as though he couldn't believe his eyes brought her to life with a rude awakening.

Charles was sitting at a table a few feet away. He was accompanied by a man with a red neck and crinkly dark hair thinning drastically on top.

The balding man, who had his back to them, was talking animatedly, hitting the table with the side of his hand to emphasise some point he was making.

As they drew level, his eyes still fixed on them, Charles rose to his feet like an automaton, while his companion stopped talking and glanced up at them.

'Raynor,' Ryan nodded politely.

'Falconer,' Charles acknowledged stiffly.

'As you were otherwise engaged,' Ryan said easily, 'I thought I'd take Virginia out for lunch.'

Turning a stricken, accusing look on his bride-to-be, Charles said, 'I understood you were staying at home.'

'I intended to,' she began, 'but—'

'I can be very...persuasive,' Ryan broke in, giving her a smiling, sidelong glance. A glance that made them conspirators. 'Can't I, my love?'

Watching Charles freeze at the endearment, and knowing

his companion was listening to every word, she stammered, 'I—I...'

Ryan squeezed her arm. 'It took a little time, but when I—'

Terrified he was going to explain exactly what methods of persuasion he had used, she broke in hurriedly, 'Shouldn't we be going?'

'You're quite right, we should,' he said at once. Then addressing the two men, 'My apologies gentlemen, for interrupting your lunch.'

A second or two later, Ryan's proprietorial arm around her waist, she was being swept through the door. Glancing back over her shoulder she saw that Charles was still on his feet, swaying a little like some punch-drunk boxer.

Dazed and incapable of coherent thought, she felt very much the same.

While the lift, containing perhaps half a dozen people, carried them smoothly downwards, she struggled to take in what had happened, all the implications of that awkward little scene, and what had gone before.

The question of why Ryan had pressured her into lunching at Moonrakers, and why he'd kissed her in such a public place, was now answered. Somehow he had known that Charles would be there and, intent on causing trouble, had staged the whole thing.

Brilliantly.

He had manipulated her with consummate skill. Even his timing had been superb, but then, she had always been aware that he was a first-rate tactician, a master of strategy.

Remembering Charles's accusing look, she knew she must have appeared more than willing to be there. Exactly how Ryan had wanted her to appear, she realised bitterly, as she recalled his arm around her waist, his little conspiratorial glance, the way he'd squeezed her arm, his endearment...

As soon as they were out in the sunshine, she turned on

him fiercely. 'You're a rotten, miserable, unscrupulous, bast—'

A finger placed on her lips stopped the outburst.

'Two many people about,' he said calmly, 'If you want to hurl abuse at me we'd better take a walk in the park.'

The limousine was drawn up by the kerb, the chauffeur standing by.

'Drop us at the nearest entrance to Kenelm Park, please, Maxwell,' Ryan instructed, and handed her in.

While they drove the short distance, Virginia sat tight-lipped silence, furious with Ryan, but equally furious with herself for not having guessed what he was up to, and somehow preventing it.

As they drew up alongside the elaborate Victorian gates that marked the main entrance to the park, Ryan said, 'You can take the rest of the afternoon off, Maxwell. We won't be needing you.'

A broad grin spreading across his face, the man said gratefully, 'Thanks, Mr Falconer.'

Jumping out, Ryan offered Virginia his hand.

Face set, she ignored it.

The intended rebuff was spoilt when she stumbled, and only Ryan's prompt action saved her from falling.

Holding her unnecessarily close, he observed with a smugness that grated on her raw nerves, 'That's what comes of trying to be too independent. It's a good thing I was there to help you.'

Jerking herself free, she headed blindly for the tall black-and-gold wrought iron gates which still incorporated an old-fashioned turnstile.

The park was green and bathed in sunshine and, following the lunch-time invasion, relatively deserted.

Selecting a sun-dappled spot beneath the trees, Ryan turned to face her and invited, 'Okay, let it fly.'

Bristling with barely contained fury, she accused

hoarsely, 'You staged the whole thing just to cause trouble! Don't try and deny it.'

'I wasn't going to. I'm quite pleased by how well it worked.'

Helplessly, she said, 'I don't see how you knew he'd be there...'

'Simple. His companion, who arranged the time and place, was in my pay.'

Ryan's calm admission brought a fresh surge of anger. 'You're loathsome and despicable—'

Looking amused, he said, 'While your choice of adjectives is quite wide, you've forgotten vile and contemptible—'

Virginia, who had never in her life struck a blow in anger, and hadn't thought herself capable of it, saw red. Without conscious volition she swung her hand and smacked his face with enough force to jerk his head sideways.

Palm tingling, suddenly horrified by what she'd done, she stared aghast at the dusky red mark her hand had left on his lean, tanned cheek.

With long fingers, he touched the spot tenderly, and winced.

'You're only trying to make me feel bad,' she said thickly.

'And you don't?'

'Yes, I do,' she admitted miserably and, though she hadn't meant to, found herself apologising. 'I'm sorry...'

'I guess I asked for it. Though I've still no intention of allowing you to slap me and get away with it scot-free.'

As she stepped back, scared by the menacing gleam in his eyes, he added, 'Don't get the wrong idea, I've never struck a woman, and I don't intend to start now. But there are other ways...'

Panic-stricken, she turned to run, but he caught her arm and spun her round. A moment later she found herself amongst the shrubbery, her back against a tree. 'More enjoyable ways,' he finished softly.

Despite her attempts to free herself, one hand behind her head, he plundered her mouth, while his other hand undid the buttons of her blouse and slipped inside to find her breast.

When he began to tease the nipple through the flimsy material of her bra, terrified of where it might be leading, she attempted to bring her knee up, as she had been taught in a self-defence class.

He neatly blocked the move and, in retaliation, nipped her lower lip between his teeth, just hard enough to make her give up any further attempt to fight back and freeze into stillness.

'That's better,' he murmured and, using lips and tongue and experienced fingers, soon had her mindless with wanting.

She was dazed, knocked completely off balance, when he finally called a halt and, having deftly rebuttoned her blouse, drew her clear of the shrubbery and back onto the path, tucking her hand beneath his arm.

The whole thing was effected so smoothly that, by the time a woman walking a white miniature poodle approached, apart from Virginia's hectic flush, they showed no sign of doing anything more unseemly than taking a stroll.

'Fancy a coffee? Or an ice cream?' Ryan asked. He sounded infuriatingly cool and casual, as if nothing at all had happened.

In spite of the adrenalin pumping through her veins, Virginia felt incapable of either fight or flight. 'I'd like a coffee, please.' She tried to emulate his careless tone and failed singularly.

'Then let's carry on to The Hungry Hippo. There's an exciting choice between plastic cups and thick pottery mugs, but the coffee's some of the best I've ever had in London.'

The Hungry Hippo was a small, open-air snack bar on the edge of the park. It boasted a blue awning with a picture of a pink and cavernously yawning hippo, rickety plastic chairs, and tables with wobbly umbrellas, several of which were vacant.

Choosing one slightly apart from the rest, Ryan settled Virginia into a chair and mounted the steps to the wooden hut.

Sitting limply in the sun, she watched him lean his elbows on the counter while he chatted with the woman who appeared to be in charge of the coffee machine.

Though middle-aged and matronly, she was clearly affected by his charm, and kept patting her tightly permed hair into place as she served him.

When he returned he was carrying two blue pottery mugs adorned with pink hippos. Placing one in front of Virginia, he remarked, 'The coffee here is piping hot, and I've discovered through trial and error that the mugs are preferable to getting one's fingers scalded.'

A cautious sip proved the coffee was every bit as good as he'd said. Even so, it was an unlikely place for a multi-millionaire to frequent and, puzzled, she commented, 'You sound as if you come here often.'

'I've been a few times,' he admitted idly. 'I'm staying at the Kenelm Mayfair. Kenelm Park is handy for a spot of morning exercise, and the snack bar opens early for coffee.'

Frowning, she asked, 'How long have you been in London?'

'Ten days or so, this time.'

This time...

Answering that unspoken thought, he said, 'I've been over several times just lately.'

With a sudden unease, she wondered why.

Her voice studiously casual, she asked, 'On business, presumably?'

'Yes... You might even say delicate and confidential business.'

She wished desperately that he would hurry up and finish his business, whatever it was, and go back to New York.

'When do you think you'll be going home?' she asked without a great deal of hope.

'When my business is completed and I've got what I came for.'

On the surface his reply was innocent enough, yet something about the way he smiled, a certain nuance in his tone, increased her feeling of uneasiness.

Convinced it would be unwise to go any further along that track, she lapsed into silence while she finished her coffee.

As she put down her mug, with the suddenness of an ambush, Ryan said, 'You still haven't told me why you thought it necessary to leave me practically at the altar.'

'And you haven't told me why you thought it necessary to marry me in the first place.'

'You don't think it might have been because I fell head over heels in love with you?'

'No, I don't,' she said shortly, and thought, if only it had been.

A knife seemed to twist in her heart.

Unable to bear the pain, she added, 'And I don't want to talk about it. It's all over and done with. Nothing can alter the past.'

'The moving finger, and all that?'

In no mood to be drawn into a philosophical discussion, she said raggedly, 'I must go. I need to get home.'

As she started to rise he put a restraining hand on her arm. 'There's just one thing before you think of leaving. When I spoke to Raynor this morning I could hardly credit his absurd accusations. I need to hear from your own lips why you left me.'

'Because I'd no intention of letting you use me while you played around with Madeline.'

'I'd guessed it was something to do with Madeline. You were never the same after you saw her kiss me that night... But there was nothing between us, I swear.'

'She told me herself that the pair of you had been lovers... And before you bother to deny it, Janice told me the same thing.'

'It's true that Madeline and I had had a brief fling, but that was all in the past. Do you really think I'd have played around with my stepbrother's wife or cheated on you?'

'If you wanted her yourself, and he'd taken her away from you.'

'I didn't want her myself. What little there had been between us was over well before she married Steven.'

Virginia shook her head. 'She told me what your plans were, how you were marrying me so the family wouldn't suspect what was going on.'

He muttered something under his breath that sounded suspiciously like an oath. Then, with a sigh, he said, 'And you believed her.'

It was a statement, rather than a question, but she answered, 'Yes, I did. That's why I'm *never* coming back to you.'

He smiled without mirth. 'Even if you don't know the meaning of the words love and trust, I want you back Virginia, and I'll extract payment for every day you make me wait.'

His certainty sent a chill down her spine, making her shiver.

Jumping up so violently that she sent the rickety plastic chair tumbling backwards, she croaked, 'I must go.'

Rising to his feet with fluid grace, he righted the chair and said, 'I'll walk you back.'

Thrown by his sudden compliance, she found herself wondering agitatedly what he was up to.

But perhaps, satisfied that he had done enough harm for one day, he was prepared to rest on his laurels for the time being?

She could only hope so. There was still Charles to face, and she felt unable to cope with anything further.

Picking up Virginia's hand, Ryan tucked it through his arm. When she made an attempt to withdraw it, he tightened his elbow, and feeling unequal to a fight, she weakly left it where it was.

Though very conscious of the bone and muscle beneath the fine material of his sleeve, and the occasional brush of his thigh against hers as they walked, she tried to appear unaffected.

Neither of them spoke until they turned the corner into Usher Street, then Ryan broke the silence to ask, 'Not having second thoughts?'

She glanced up at him. 'About what?'

'About coming back here. It may not be wise.'

'Wise? I don't understand what you mean.'

'If Raynor turned nasty—'

'Charles hasn't a nasty bone in his body.'

'I wouldn't be too sure of that. He looked pretty upset at lunch-time.'

'He might be shocked and angry, but he would never lift a finger, if that's what you're suggesting.'

'Jealousy is a powerful emotion. It can make even the most placid people do things they would never normally dream of doing.'

Shaking her head, she said with finality, 'Charles would never do anything to harm me.'

'Are you absolutely certain of that? It might be safer to book you into a hotel.'

Knowing now that this had been carefully planned as a two-pronged attack, and Ryan was doing his utmost to scare and unsettle her, she said calmly, 'I'm absolutely certain.'

As he escorted her up the steps of number sixteen, he asked, 'What are you intending to tell him?'

'The truth, of course.'

Though it was still sunny, since they had left the park a wind had sprung up, and now it blew a tendril of brown curly hair across her cheek.

Brushing it back, he tucked it behind her ear.

That light but sure touch made her tremble.

Smiling knowingly, Ryan queried, 'The whole truth? Or an edited version of it?'

Remembering the stricken look on Charles's face, she hesitated, then said distractedly, 'I don't know. I don't want to hurt or upset him any more than I have to.'

'He really matters to you?'

'Yes, he does. He's been wonderful to me, and I care about him.'

'I'm beginning to believe you.'

It struck her that Ryan sounded more pleased than bothered.

'Perhaps I'll just tell him you coerced me.'

'Do you think he'll believe it?'

Knowing how damning the little scene must have appeared, she said with rather more confidence than she felt, 'I'm sure he will.'

Then feeling the need to fight back, she added sardonically, 'Though I must admit you engineered the whole thing quite brilliantly, I'm afraid it's been a complete waste of time and effort.'

'Not a complete waste.' A gleam in those indigo eyes, he added, 'There were parts of it I really quite enjoyed.'

'I'm afraid I can't say the same.'

With a slight shrug of his broad shoulders, Ryan queried, 'So when are you planning the wedding for?'

The sudden question took her by surprise and, without thinking, she answered, 'Next Monday.'

Only when the words were out did it occur to her that it would have made more sense to lie. That way the wedding might have been a *fait accompli* before he realised.

But now it was too late.

He raised a dark brow. 'As soon as that?'

'We have no reason to wait.'

Drily, he said, 'I can understand why Raynor's in a hurry... Or do you still intend to hold out on him?'

Her lips tightening, she said, 'No, I don't.' Then, curtly, she said, 'Now, as you have my key, would you mind letting me in?'

'Certainly.' He opened the door then dropping the key into her hand, said, 'You'd better have this back.'

'Quite sure you wouldn't like to keep it?' she asked caustically.

He grinned. 'Thanks, but that won't be necessary.' Bending his dark head he kissed her, before saying with certainty, 'Next time *you'll* come to *me.*'

She was still standing as though made of marble when he reached the bottom of the steps and turned. 'By the way, you'll find your purse on the coffee table in the living-room.'

A second later he was striding away down the street, the rising wind ruffling his dark hair.

Feeling curiously shaky, she went inside and closed the door behind her. Then grimacing at her own stupidity in locking the stable door after the horse had bolted, she put on the safety chain.

Next time you'll come to me.

If he was trying to rattle her, he'd succeeded. He'd sounded so terrifyingly confident. So sure of himself.

But she mustn't let him get to her, she told herself firmly as she went upstairs to change.

When she was dressed in trousers and a bottle-green top,

she went through to the kitchen and began to prepare the special meal she had promised Charles.

While she worked, her mind kept going over and over the day's events like a video that refused to be switched off.

Ryan's sudden appearance in the kitchen doorway; the way he had removed the sliver of glass from her foot; the methods he had used to coerce her into having lunch with him; the accusing look on Charles's face...

She groaned. Though she had tried to make light of it to Ryan, what Charles had seen that lunch-time might have done more harm to their relationship than she could ever repair.

Please, God, it hadn't, but all she could do was wait and see what his reaction was when she told him the truth. It might not be easy to convince him that Ryan had engineered the whole thing...

By half past-seven, with the dining-room table set and the coq au vin simmering in the sauté pan, unable to settle, she prowled about, restless as a cat shut in the wrong house.

Staring out of the window she saw that a front had gone through, pushing the good weather before it. A strongish wind was herding clouds like shaggy grey sheep across the sky, and it had started to rain.

At twenty-to-eight, she was spooning a creamy sauce over the prawn starter when there was the sound of a key in the lock, followed by a metallic rattle and clunk.

Hurrying through to the hall, she called, 'Just a minute.'

After a short struggle, she released the safety chain and opened the door.

'I'm sorry, I forgot I'd left it on.'

The rain was coming down in earnest now, and though the car-parking area was just down a side street, Charles's fair hair was darkened by downpour.

His face set, and offering no word of greeting, he closed the door and hung up his jacket. Then, going into the small cloakroom, he towelled his hair and ran a comb through it, while Virginia hovered helplessly in the hall.

'Charles, I need to talk to you, to explain.'

Still without a word, he followed her across the hall and into the living-room.

Her knees feeling as though they might buckle at any minute, she sank down on the couch while he remained standing.

Knowing that it wasn't going to be easy, she suggested, 'Shall we have a drink before dinner?'

'If that's what you'd like.'

He went over to the sideboard and, filling two glasses with pale dry sherry, handed her one.

She took a nervous sip that was more like a gulp, while his stayed untouched.

'Aren't you going to sit down?' she asked awkwardly when he showed no sign of joining her.

'Perhaps you'd better come straight to the point,' he said tightly. 'I presume you've decided to go back to him?'

'No!' she cried. 'No! I told you I'd *never* go back to him.'

'That wasn't the impression I got at lunch-time.'

She swallowed hard. Convincing him looked like being every bit as difficult as she'd feared.

CHAPTER EIGHT

'IT WAS the wrong impression,' she said earnestly. 'I realise what it must have looked like, but Ryan set the whole thing up to make you think that.'

It was obvious Charles didn't believe her, and her lovely eyes filled with despairing tears.

Immediately his face softened. Sitting down by her side he took her hand. 'Perhaps you'd better tell me the whole story. Why did you go to meet him in the first place?'

'I didn't go to meet him. He came here.'

'He knew where you were living?'

'That first day in the park I told him I was living with you.'

'Surely you didn't give him the exact address?'

'He already knew.'

'The devil he did!' Charles exclaimed. 'How did he know?'

'He'd had detectives looking for me ever since I left him, and somehow they'd managed to find out where I lived and worked.'

'So he came here,' Charles said slowly. 'How did he know you'd be home?'

'He said he'd been into the gallery, so I imagine he found out then.'

Charles muttered, 'Damn... Helen must have told him you weren't there before I arrived on the scene.'

He gave the hand he was holding a squeeze. 'It must have been a nasty shock when he turned up here.'

'It was.'

'Why did you let him in?'

'I wouldn't have done, but he took me by surprise and

was inside before I realised.' Her voice shook. 'I asked him what he wanted, and he said he'd come to take me out to lunch.

'At first I refused, but he wouldn't take no for an answer and, at the finish, thinking it would be better to be in a public place rather than here alone with him, I agreed to go.

'What I hadn't realised was that he intended to take me to the same restaurant as you—'

'How could he possibly have known where I'd be lunching? The only people who knew were Andrew Bish, who made the booking, and myself.'

'Andrew Bish, if that's his real name, was in Ryan's pay.' Seeing Charles looked unconvinced, she insisted, 'It's quite true, he admitted it.

'The whole thing was carefully planned and staged. That's why he kissed me; that's why he called me "my love"; he wanted you to see and think the worst.'

Blue eyes looked steadily into greeny-grey. 'Is what you've told me the truth?'

'Yes, it is.'

It was. Though not the whole truth by a long chalk.

'And you don't want to go back to him?'

'I couldn't bear to,' she said shakily.

'What about us?' Once more his nice-looking face was full of tension. 'Have you changed your mind about marrying me?'

'No. I still want to marry you. If you haven't changed your mind,' she added uncertainly.

His answer was to pull her to him and hold her as if he'd never let her go.

It was such a relief to see joy replace that look of strain, to be held and cradled in the warmth of his arms, that it wasn't until a faint smell of burning came drifting in that she recalled the meal waiting on the stove.

'Oh, dear!' Pulling herself free, she scrambled to her feet. 'I forgot all about the coq au vin.'

Following her through to the kitchen, he said, 'Don't worry, if it's spoilt we'll have a meal out. There's plenty to celebrate.'

'I think it's just caught, rather than spoilt. Come and have a taste and see what you think.'

She spooned up a little of the sauce and offered it to him.

'Mmm... Much too good to waste. We'll eat out another night.'

They began their meal in a silence, both relieved and thankful that what might have been a serious breakup had ended with even greater understanding.

After a while, her thoughts straying to the business appointment Charles had described as 'important', and how he'd said with unusual animation, 'If all goes well, it should mean a virtual end to my financial problems', she wondered how it had turned out.

Then recalling his, 'There's plenty to celebrate', and sensing an undercurrent of excitement in her usually phlegmatic companion, she asked hopefully, 'Did everything go well this evening?'

'Very well. I would have told you at once, only the whole thing's been overshadowed by more important issues.'

'Tell me now,' she suggested with a smile.

'I'll give you one guess.'

'You've had a find?' In the art world there was always the possibility of coming across something that would mean big money.

'You could say that. Just over a week ago I received a phone call offering me a Roisser...'

'A *Roisser*?'

'I could hardly believe it either. Still, I agreed to take a look at it. The caller, who identified himself as Mr Smith, insisted on the greatest secrecy, so I made an appointment for him to bring the painting over the following evening when the gallery was closed.'

'And?' Virginia prompted eagerly.

'I was quite certain it was genuine.'

'Was it signed?'

'Only with an elongated R. But that's how Roisser often signed his work. It's as distinctive as his brushwork. His two most famous paintings, *Dragonflies*, and *Midsummer*, that hang in the Louvre, are signed that way.'

'So which one was this?'

'*Footprints.*'

Her jaw dropped. *Footprints* was recognised as one of Gerard Roisser's masterpieces.

'But surely that went to the States in the early nineteen-seventies and disappeared into the Jefferson family's private art collection?'

'You're absolutely right, it did. However, earlier this year the painting was purchased from a Mr Otis Jefferson of New York.'

With a stirring of unease, she asked, 'But if everything was quite above board, why the need for all the secrecy?'

Not one to be rushed, Charles began the story in his own precise way. 'The young man who wanted to sell it had recently inherited his godfather's estate in Kent.

'He'd borrowed heavily on his expectations, but unfortunately for him there was very little money, only a mouldering pile of a house, and a collection of pictures.

'Because he didn't want his titled family, and his wife in particular, to know he had extensive gambling debts, he was desperate to raise some money without "causing a stink," as he put it.

'None of the family were art lovers and, realising that one picture out of so many was unlikely to be missed, he decided to sell the Roisser. Not only was it the most valuable but, as his godfather had suffered a stroke shortly after its purchase, it had never even been hung.

'Because he needed the money urgently, he was prepared to part with it for considerably less than it was worth. His only stipulation was cash in hand, and the whole thing kept a complete secret.'

'But doesn't a deal of that kind create all sorts of...problems?'

'Yes, it does,' Charles admitted frankly. 'Apart from the fact that it isn't easy to raise a very large amount of ready cash, it means the painting has to be passed on in the same shady way.'

'But you've never countenanced anything like that,' she said desperately. 'And there's the good reputation of the gallery to think about.'

'Yes, I know. That's why, if things hadn't been so difficult, I would have had nothing to do with it.'

Virginia felt her nerves tighten. Charles had always been strictly law-abiding. His financial troubles must be a great deal worse than he had admitted if he would allow himself to be pushed into taking that kind of risk.

Carefully, she said, 'You're talking as if you're planning to go ahead with the deal?'

He grimaced. 'I know exactly what you're thinking. It must sound like utter madness. But it's not as if I'm doing any real harm, and it will solve nearly all my problems.'

Afraid for him, she protested, 'Isn't the whole thing far too risky? Suppose it got out?'

'There's not much chance of that. Mr Smith isn't likely to blab, and I presume I can rely on you to say nothing?'

'Of course you can.'

He patted her hand. 'That's my girl.'

Deciding to try the down-to-earth approach, she objected, 'But if you're already in financial difficulties I don't see how you can hope to raise what you've just admitted is a very large amount of ready cash.'

'I've already solved that. I found a source that will give me a short-term loan using the business as collateral.'

She blanched. 'Are you absolutely certain the painting's genuine? Supposing this is just a clever con?'

'I'd stake my life that it's a genuine Roisser. But to be on the safe side I contacted Otis Jefferson and, though he wouldn't tell me the name of the buyer, he confirmed that last year he'd sold *Footprints* to another collector.'

'But suppose this Mr Smith showed you the genuine Roisser and then—'

'My dear girl,' Charles protested mildly, 'do you take me for a fool? I'm well aware that a last minute switch could be made, that's why I refused to let the painting out of my hands. It's been locked in our strongroom since that first night.'

Virginia played her last card. 'I know there are always some of the more unscrupulous dealers or private collectors who will buy without asking too many questions, but it might take a long time to find one who—'

'I had a buyer, a private collector named Anderson, already lined up.'

'You've already found a buyer?' she echoed stupidly.

'If I hadn't had a buyer waiting, I couldn't have afforded to take the risk.'

That sounded more like Charles the businessman, and she breathed a sigh of relief.

Leaning over the table, he patted her hand reassuringly. 'Don't worry, my dear. Everything has gone through smoothly. Tonight I handed over the picture and got my money back, plus a very handsome profit. We'll be starting our married life nicely solvent, rather than in the red.'

She smiled, wanting to be happy for him, but at the back of her mind was a nagging doubt as to the wisdom of it.

Yet if the transaction had already gone through, and the new owner was happy, what could possibly go wrong?

After the meal, which Charles pronounced excellent, he

helped her wash the dishes and, because of the change in the weather, lit a fire.

At ease together, the rest of the evening was spent in the aura of cosy domesticity that had grown up over the past months.

Only when bedtime approached and they mounted the stairs together, as they had done many times before, did Virginia start to feel uncomfortable. What if Charles wanted her to sleep with him?

If he did, this time she must go ahead and do it. Yet even as she made up her mind, she was aware of a strange feeling of reluctance.

It was all Ryan's fault, she told herself vexedly. Once he had gone back to the States, and she and Charles were married, everything would be fine. But for the moment he had totally unsettled her.

Either reading her mind, or perhaps remembering her coolness of the previous night and losing confidence, Charles said, 'There's nothing I'd like better than to take you to bed, but I know you've had an upsetting time lately, so I won't press you... After all it's less than a week to our wedding day.'

Stooping, he kissed her chastely on the cheek.

She kissed him back, gratefully.

If he had hoped for a different response, he hid it well.

'Good night then. If you want to sleep in tomorrow, I'll try not to disturb you...'

Virginia shook her head, 'I've decided to go into work as usual.'

'Don't let what happened today throw you. Now you're on your guard you could always keep the chain on the door.'

But recalling Ryan's parting words, 'Next time you'll come to me,' she felt convinced that he would come to neither Usher Street nor the gallery.

'No, I'll go into work with you.' Carefully, she added, 'At least we'll be together.'

Charles looked gratified.

For the next two or three days life regained some semblance of peace as she and Charles went back to their ordinary routine.

Each morning they drove to the gallery and passed the day working as usual, before returning home to cook a meal and spend a quiet evening together. And each night they went upstairs and parted to go into their respective rooms with nothing further being said, and no more than a light kiss on the cheek or forehead.

But, in spite of the outward normality, Virginia felt restless and on edge, stuck on hold.

Though there was no sign of Ryan, she couldn't believe he had given up so easily, and waiting for him to make his next move was like waiting for the second shoe to drop.

He couldn't seriously expect her to go to him.

Or could he?

It was the not knowing that got to her. The fear of what he might be planning. A fear that lurked at the back of her mind like a dark shadow during the day, and woke her, palpitating, from sleep in the middle of the night.

The worst part was trying to hide it from Charles. He seemed to be on a high, happy that his mounting debts had been paid off, and confident that Ryan had given up and was going to leave them alone.

But then, of course, she had kept a large part of the truth from him, and he didn't know Ryan as well as she did.

As the wedding day approached, rather than fading away, Virginia's anxiety intensified, until she was practically living on her nerves, only waiting for the whole thing to be over.

Once they were on their honeymoon, she comforted herself repeatedly, she would be safe from Ryan and able to relax.

At Charles's insistence they were closing the gallery for the day on Monday, so that Helen could come to the wedding.

Guessing how the other woman felt about him, Virginia had been doubtful whether she would want to come.

But Helen had accepted the invitation with a smile and, hiding her lovelorn state behind a resolutely cheerful façade, had assured them that as it would be mid-week when they were away, if she just had someone who could sit behind the reception desk, she could easily hold the fort.

Some temporary help had been arranged, and after the ceremony the newly-weds were due to fly to Paris.

'Four days should allow enough time to take my wife trousseau shopping on the Champs Elysées,' Charles remarked, as he sat on the edge of Virginia's desk, 'and we'll have a longer honeymoon later.'

Seeing the shadow hadn't lifted from her face, he squeezed her hand and said seriously, 'Don't you think it's time you stopped worrying about Falconer? If he was planning to try any more tricks he would have already done so. In all probability he's gone back home by now.

'Tell you what, I'll check. I have his hotel phone number in my office.' Charles hurried away.

He was back almost immediately, a smile of satisfaction on his face. 'Just as I thought, he left for the States first thing Wednesday morning.'

'He *did*?'

'The hotel clerk was quite certain.'

Mingled with Virginia's relief was a feeling of incredulity that Ryan had given up so easily.

The following day was Saturday, always the busiest day at the gallery. But because—almost as if she were superstitious—Virginia had so far bought nothing new for the wedding, Charles insisted on her taking as much time off as she needed.

'Go and buy a nice new outfit, and some pretty undies, and have a leisurely lunch in Harrods.'

Smiling, she set out to do his bidding but, anxious not to be too long, she ate an early lunch and, dropping her purchases at home on the way, took a taxi back to the gallery.

She was surprised to find that Charles had gone out.

'He wouldn't have left just Moira and me,' Helen explained, 'only it was something that needed his attention and couldn't wait. He said he'd be back as soon as possible.'

In the event he was absent for the entire afternoon, so Virginia saw nothing of him until just before it was time to go home, when he appeared at her office door looking rushed and harassed.

'I'm afraid I have to go straight out again. Do you mind locking up for me and making your own way home?'

'Of course not. Is everything all right?'

'Something rather urgent has cropped up. I have to go to Sussex.'

'Shall I hold dinner for you?'

He shook his head. 'I'll be out for dinner.' Then, with an attempt at a smile, he added, 'I've no idea what time I'll get back, so don't wait up for me.'

A moment later he was gone.

Frowning at the closed door, she wondered what could have happened to throw the usually unflappable Charles out of his normal, calm routine.

Trying to subdue a sudden rush of foreboding, she told herself it was probably just something he needed to deal with before Monday, but the feeling of impending disaster lingered, refusing to be banished.

When she had taken her duplicate set of keys from her desk, she went down to make the usual security checks and ascertain that every member of the public had left the gallery.

Moira, the young art student who came in to help on Saturdays, had already gone, and the only person still there was Helen.

'Charles looked worried to death when he got back,' she said, her nice hazel eyes anxious, 'and he was acting strangely.'

'In what way?' Virginia asked.

'A man who had just bought a Jules Pesaro wanted to ask his advice about a frame, but he virtually brushed him off. Said he had to go straight out again. It's so unlike Charles to be rude to the customers...'

Wanting to reassure the other woman, but unable to, Virginia admitted, 'All he told me was that something urgent had cropped up, and he'd like me to lock the gallery.'

'Do you need any help?'

'No, thanks. I've done all the checks, so you may as well go.'

As Helen was about to pull on her coat, the phone on the reception desk rang. Lifting the receiver, she said, 'The Charles Raynor Gallery. Yes... Yes, she's still here.' Then, to Virginia, she said 'It's for you.'

'Hello?'

Without preamble, Ryan laid it on the line. 'I'll be going back to New York tomorrow and I want you to come with me.'

Watching all the colour drain from the younger woman's face, and concerned for her, Helen pushed the chair closer.

Sinking limply into it, Virginia said, 'I thought you'd already gone home.'

'That was just a flying visit; now I'm back at the Kenelm Mayfair. I'm in the Imperial Suite, and I shall expect you to join me there tonight.'

'Well you'll be disappointed,' she told him hoarsely.

Infuriatingly calm, he disagreed, 'I don't think so. You'll come if you care about Raynor.'

There was silence while the threat, and it was a threat, drip-fed itself into her befuddled brain. Then she stammered, 'W-what?'

'I said, you'll come if you care about Raynor... And don't forget I want you there *tonight*. No matter how late it is, I'll send a car for you. You'd better write down the phone number and ring me when you're ready to come.'

With a feeling of inevitability, and knowing Ryan never made empty threats, she picked up a pen, and her unsteady fingers hardly able to control it, wrote down the number he gave her.

'By the way, don't bother to pack more than a few overnight essentials,' he added, 'you can buy everything you need in New York.'

The line went dead.

For a moment or two she sat staring blindly at the number on the pad until the figures seemed burnt into her brain. Then, making a great effort to gather herself, she replaced the receiver.

'Are you all right?' Helen wanted to know. 'You've gone as white as a sheet.'

'Yes, I'm all right,' Virginia lied through stiff lips. 'It was just a bit of a shock. I thought he was in the States.'

Her hazel eyes curious, Helen said, 'It was the man who's been into the gallery a couple of times this last week, wasn't it? Ryan Falconer. As well as being attractive, his voice is very distinctive...

'The last time he came in, the day you weren't here, Charles took him into his office. Though neither of them raised their voices, my guess is they had a real set to.'

When Virginia made no comment, Helen went on, 'Though he's absolutely gorgeous—those eyes—I should imagine he can be quite formidable.'

'Yes, he can.'

After hovering for a moment or two, seeing the younger woman wasn't about to elaborate, Helen said, 'Well if there's nothing I can do for you, I'd best be getting off.'

She pulled on her coat and picked up her bag. 'I'll see you at the church on Monday.' Her voice wasn't quite steady.

On an impulse, Virginia asked, 'You love Charles, don't you?'

Flushing, the older woman said defensively, 'Whatever gave you that idea?'

'You do, don't you?' Virginia persisted.

'Yes,' Helen admitted quietly. 'But don't think for a minute that I—'

'I'm not jealous,' Virginia denied quickly. 'I was just asking, because he may need your support...'

'*My* support?'

'And if he does, I'd like him to have it.'

Just for an instant, hazel eyes met grey-green and held. Then Helen nodded and, putting the strap of her bag over her shoulder, made her way to the door.

Virginia followed and, having locked up after her, set the security-alarm system before leaving by the back way.

After a couple of days of cool, unsettled weather, it was once again warm and sunny and, accompanied by a sensation of *déjà vu*, she walked home through the park.

The house, when she reached it, was empty and waiting. The shopping she had dumped on the couch earlier had a forlorn, abandoned air.

Carrying the packages up to her room, Virginia put them on the chest of drawers and, without taking a second look at the contents, went downstairs again.

For the moment she felt oddly calm, suspended in time, like a victim with her head on the block, just waiting for the axe to fall.

She prepared and ate a solitary meal, hoping it would

take away the hollow feeling, then washed the dishes before going through to the living-room.

The house felt oddly empty, and she found herself listening to the silence. Making an effort at normality she switched on the television, but after a while the silence seemed preferable.

Left alone with her thoughts, and beset once more by gnawing worries and unanswerable questions, the evening crawled past on leaden feet.

When Charles had failed to return by nine-thirty, Virginia, who had slept badly the last few nights, went upstairs, weary and emotionally exhausted.

Hoping against hope that Ryan had been bluffing, but convinced all the same that he hadn't, she showered, cleaned her teeth, and prepared for bed.

Leaving the bedroom door open so she would be sure to hear Charles come home, she snuggled down to try to get some sleep.

But once beneath the duvet, she tossed and turned restlessly, unable to settle. Finally giving up the attempt, she switched on the bedside lamp again and picked up a book.

While she forced her eyes to read the print, her brain stubbornly refused to take it in, and she found herself repeatedly rereading the same page.

It was almost eleven when she finally heard the front door open and close. For what seemed an age she sat waiting for Charles to come up to bed.

When he didn't, she pulled on her dressing gown, knotted the sash, and in her bare feet went quietly down the stairs.

The hall and the living-room were in darkness, but there was a rectangle of light spilling from the open doorway of the kitchen.

Moving silently to the threshold, she looked in.

Charles was slumped in a chair by the table, his shoulders bowed, his fair head supported in his hands. He looked prematurely old, as if life had suddenly defeated him.

As she hesitated in the doorway, he glanced up and saw her.

She watched him straighten his shoulders, watched his attempt to return to the quietly confident man she knew, and her heart swelled with sympathy and affection for him.

Sliding into the seat opposite, she reached across and took his hand. It felt icy cold.

'I wondered why you weren't coming to bed.'

'I was thinking of having some cocoa.' Even his voice sounded beaten.

'I'll heat some milk.' She jumped to her feet, glad to have something positive to do.

When she had made two cups of milky cocoa, she put one in front of him, and sat down opposite again.

While, fair head bent, he spooned sugar into his cocoa and stirred it as if his very life depended on it, she jumped in at the deep end.

'I know something's terrible wrong. Won't you please tell me what it is?'

He picked up his cocoa and put it down again untasted.

'The Roisser I bought...'

Backed into a corner by her fears, she waited for what she was now certain was coming.

'It's a worthless copy,' Charles said flatly. 'A brilliant fake. I know Roisser's work and I could have staked my life it was absolutely genuine.'

Her voice commendably steady, she asked, 'How did you discover it wasn't?'

'Anderson rang me up at lunch-time in an absolute frenzy. A chance remark made by someone in the know had convinced him that another collector had the real *Footprints*.

'He made further careful enquiries and discovered that the painting is in Sir Humphrey Post's private collection, and has been ever since he bought it from Otis Jefferson last year.'

'There's no way he could be wrong?' Virginia asked without much hope.

'That was my first thought. So, to be on the safe side, I discreetly approached both Sir Humphrey Post and Otis Jefferson.

'Having obtained Sir Humphrey's permission, Jefferson confirmed that Post was the man he'd sold *Footprints* to.

'Though I hadn't told him the full story by any means, Sir Humphrey, who apparently knows the gallery and its reputation, was very cooperative. He invited me to have dinner at Ferndale Manor, his home in Sussex, and see the painting for myself...

'There's not a shadow of doubt that he has the authentic *Footprints*, with its completed provenance.'

'What about Mr Smith?'

'As you might expect,' Charles said bitterly, 'the telephone number he gave me in case I needed to contact him is no longer in use.'

'And the man you sold the copy to? Anderson?'

'If only I could return his money, the whole thing could be hushed up and my reputation saved. But I can't... And if he doesn't get every penny back by Monday, he's threatening to call in the police.

'I've been the world's worst fool. I'll lose the gallery and everything I own, and it's odds-on I'll end up in prison.'

As Charles's despairing words echoed through her head they were replaced by Ryan's. 'You'll come if you care about Raynor...'

Somehow he had known what was going to happen, and was offering a way out... *So long as she went back to him...*

Icy cold and calm, her thinking swift and lucid, she asked, 'How much money do you need?'

He named a staggering sum.

With a feeling of inevitability, Virginia went through to the hall and rang the number that was branded on her mind.

When Ryan's voice answered, she said stonily, 'I'm ready to come.'

'How much does Raynor need?'

She told him.

Without the slightest hesitation, he said, 'Maxwell will bring a cheque.'

'When will you want the money back?'

'I won't. This is a one-off payment to provide Raynor with a fresh start, and give me what I want.'

Glancing through the kitchen door on her way to the stairs, she saw that Charles was sitting exactly as she'd left him. He didn't appear to have even noticed her absence.

After she had dressed again, she pushed a few essentials into an overnight case, as Ryan had instructed, and fastened it.

Catching sight of the packages abandoned on the chest of drawers, she thought with bitter irony that running away and leaving her wedding things behind was getting to be a habit.

When she had made her way downstairs once more, she put her case and bag in the hall and faced the hardest task of all.

Charles was still sitting staring blindly into space, sunk in a stupor of despair. Standing by his side, she put her hand on his shoulder.

He glanced up. His blue eyes were curiously blank and unfocussed, as if he were looking inward, rather than at her.

'I want to talk to you.'

'Can't it wait 'til morning?' Even his speech was slightly slurred.

'No, it can't.' Afraid for him, she shook his arm.

As though he'd made a great effort, his gaze came into

focus. 'Of course... Don't worry, I'll cancel the wedding. I wouldn't expect any woman to tie herself to a penniless gaolbird.'

'You won't be a penniless gaolbird,' she said firmly. 'Ryan's prepared to cover the amount you need. Tomorrow you'll be able to give Anderson back every penny of his money.'

It took a moment or two to sink in, then Charles shook his head as if to clear his brain. 'What did you say?'

She repeated it.

Sounding dazed, he said, 'When did you ask him?'

'I spoke to him on the phone a few minutes ago. But I didn't ask him. He offered.'

'How soon does he want it back?' Charles queried thickly.

'He doesn't want it back.'

'*That* amount of money? He *must* want it back!'

She shook her head, adding quickly, 'Don't worry, he can afford it. He probably gives a lot more than that to charity.'

'Why would Falconer help me out? It's not as if we're friends...'

It was the question she had been dreading.

CHAPTER NINE

AS SHE hesitated, wondering how best to break it to him, he said violently, 'No! You told me you'd never go back to him, and I won't allow you to sell yourself to save me.'

'I'm doing nothing of the kind.'

Then, knowing that somehow she must convince him, otherwise he would refuse Ryan's help, she said, 'Look, I wouldn't dream of going back to him simply for the money, but—'

'But you can't bear the thought of marrying a bankrupt? I don't blame you...'

'Please will you stop interrupting and *listen* to me? If you hadn't a penny, and you did have to go to prison, I'd still marry you if I really loved you...'

Almost matter-of-factly, as if he'd always secretly known it, he said, 'But you don't.'

'Not enough,' she admitted.

'Perhaps I always knew I was living in a fool's paradise, but I didn't want to admit it.'

'I wanted to love you. I tried to love you...'

He sighed deeply. 'It's still Falconer you care about, isn't it?'

'Yes.'

'Though you tried to deny it, I think I've always known it. I've been trying to tell myself I was mistaken, but that day in the restaurant, when he kissed you, it was painfully obvious.'

'I'm sorry.'

'And we were so close to being married.'

'It would have been a mistake,' she said with conviction. 'I'm not saying we couldn't have made it work, but it wouldn't have been fair to you. I would have been short-changing you.

'You should have a wife who loves you with passion, a wife who feels about you the way I feel about Ryan.'

'Are you going back to him?'

'Yes.'

'For good?'

'For as long as he wants me.'

'You said you didn't want to go back.'

'I didn't.' She was unable to repress a shiver. 'But I find I can't help myself.'

Charles was no fool and, after a moment, he stated, 'So when you told him I was in a mess, he offered his help, with strings, and that's when you decided to go back to him.'

'No, you're wrong.'

'It's no use,' he said tiredly. 'I know you're only doing it for me.'

Feeling as if she was picking her way through a minefield, she repeated, 'You're wrong! I'm going back to him because I *want* to.

'I'd already decided before I even knew what kind of a mess you were in... I was waiting to tell you.'

He sat up straighter. 'You say you'd made up your mind *before* you knew about my problems?'

'Yes.'

'So when did you talk to him about it?'

On safer ground now, she answered, 'He's back in London, and he rang me up at the gallery just after you'd gone. He's flying home again tomorrow, and he wants me to go with him.'

Seeing Charles wasn't altogether convinced, Virginia added, 'Ask Helen if you don't believe me. She answered the phone and recognised his voice...'

The doorbell pealed through her words. 'This will be

Ryan's chauffeur. He's bringing a cheque, and taking me back with him.'

She hurried to the door to find Maxwell standing on the step.

Handing her a white envelope, he said, 'Mr Falconer asked me to give you this, and wait for you.'

'Thank you. If you'll be kind enough to put my case in the car I'll be out in just a minute.'

'Certainly, miss.'

She took the envelope back to the kitchen and put it into Charles's hand.

He tore it open and looked at the cheque.

His face showed a strange mixture of awe and relief and anxiety. 'Falconer's actually rounded it up by several hundred thousand. He's either extremely generous, or he rates you very highly.'

Then, urgently, he asked, 'Are you really *sure* you want to go back to him?'

'Quite sure.'

'You said he only wanted you back because there was a score to settle.'

She answered with care. 'That might still be true, but, no matter how tough the going is, I'd sooner live with Ryan than without him.'

'Rather than put you at risk I'm more than willing to tear this cheque up and take my chances.'

Gambling, she said, 'You can if you like, but I shall go back to Ryan anyway.'

Watching him waver, she added, 'Now you know how things stand, unless your pride won't let you keep it, it would be a waste to tear it up...'

'The money isn't important compared to—'

'Oh, but it is,' she broke in. 'Not only does it save you, it also saves me. You see it enables me to leave you without feeling too guilty. If it hadn't been for the money I couldn't have gone back with Ryan and left you to face ruin on your own.'

She touched his cheek with her hand. 'You're one of the nicest people I've ever met, and I'd be very grateful to have you for a friend.'

'But not for a lover.' There was an edge of bitterness to his tone.

'The way I feel about Ryan precludes that. I tried to tell myself that after we were married the sexual side would come right, but I know now it never would have. And it would have been my fault. The passion was missing.'

He managed a wry smile. 'I can only feel sorry about that.'

'You'll make some lucky woman a wonderful lover—someone like Helen, who *does* love you passionately.'

She saw the surprise on his face. Clearly he had had no idea.

Perhaps she shouldn't have said anything. But possibly the knowledge would make him look at the other woman with new eyes, and if he could once see how very attractive she was...

'And speaking of Helen,' Virginia went on casually, 'perhaps she would be kind enough to help you pack up the things I've left, and take them to a charity shop.'

Stooping, she kissed his forehead. 'Thank you for being here for me when I needed you most.'

'Virginia...'

She was at the door when he spoke her name, and she stopped and turned.

'If things don't work out, I still will be here for you, even if it's only as a friend.'

'Thank you.' She smiled and blew him a kiss before gathering up her bag and letting herself quietly out of the house.

The journey through the late-Saturday-night traffic was a slow one, but Virginia scarcely noticed. Drained and empty, she sat staring straight ahead with sightless eyes, like a zombie who could neither think nor feel.

When they reached the Kenelm Mayfair, Maxwell jumped out and, carrying her case, escorted her up to the Imperial Suite.

Ryan opened the door himself, clad only in a short silk robe and, taking the case, said, 'Thank you, Maxwell. Sorry to have kept you up so late.' A generous tip changed hands. 'Goodnight.'

'Thank you, Mr Falconer. Goodnight... Goodnight, miss.'

Once inside, Ryan dropped the case and studied Virginia's pale, drawn face. 'You look absolutely shattered. Straight to bed, I think. We'll leave the talking until morning.'

His dark hair was still damp from the shower, and he was freshly shaved. He'd always been punctilious about shaving at night, aware of what damage stubble could do to a delicate skin.

He led the way through to a bedroom decorated in smoke-grey and misty-blue. There was a large bed, the duvet turned down ready.

All at once she found herself remembering clearly what he'd said in the park. 'Now I've found you, I want you in my bed. I want to make love to you until you're begging for mercy and I'm sated. Then I want to start all over again.'

A shudder ran through her.

She had put so much effort into convincing Charles that it was what she wanted to do, that she hadn't paused to reconsider all the consequences.

But perhaps that was just as well. If she had, she might have got cold feet.

Now here she was, and it was much too late for second thoughts.

If he'd cared about her in the slightest... But he didn't. He just wanted to make her suffer for leaving him.

And it could only get worse. Once they were back in the States it would mean additional pain and humiliation. She would become his whipping boy while Madeline looked on and enjoyed the spectacle.

But somehow, until his need for revenge had been met and he tired of her, she would have to cope...

'Let me help you,' Ryan's voice cut through her bleak and unhappy thoughts. 'You look about out on your feet.'

He began to undress her, neatly and methodically. When he unfastened her bra, she crossed her arms over her chest in an age-old gesture of modesty.

'Something wrong?' he asked.

Shivering, she answered, 'I haven't unpacked my nightdress.'

'You won't need it.' A faintly amused look on his face, he added, 'It isn't cold in here, and I've seen you naked before.'

But not for a long time. It was like beginning all over anew on a relationship that this time she could only dread. Already she was starting to tremble with the thought of what lay ahead.

While her treacherous body would no doubt respond and enjoy what was happening, her mind would stand aloof, hating the enslavement of her senses, but powerless to do anything about it.

It would have been infinitely preferable if she could have rejected him with both her mind and body and, because she had no choice, merely *endured* what was happening to her.

But she knew only too well that that wasn't possible.

If it had been, she saw with sudden insight, Ryan wouldn't have wanted her on those terms. He wasn't the kind of man who would be satisfied to make love to a truly unwilling woman.

Not even because she owed him.

'Hadn't you better jump in?'

His question startled her. She had been unconsciously waiting for him to pick her up and throw her on the bed like some triumphant conqueror.

She climbed in reluctantly and pulled up the duvet.

A moment later he discarded his robe, switched out the light, and slid in beside her.

When he turned and took her in his arms, she made a small, despairing sound in her throat. But all he did was draw her shivering body against the naked warmth of his, and settle her head on the comfortable junction between chest and shoulder.

She was so wound up, that it took her a second or two to appreciate that, because of her obvious exhaustion, Ryan wasn't going to make love to her.

But if she had been thinking straight, she would have realised that Ryan hadn't undressed her like an eager lover, but rather as a parent might undress a tired child.

It seemed strange to be held once again, and at first she lay stiffly, listening to the strong beat of his heart beneath her cheek.

Then gradually she relaxed, and by the time she drifted off, her mind befuddled with sleep, lying in his arms seemed like coming home after a long and desolate journey.

Drifting to the surface, half asleep and half awake, she lay relaxed and refreshed, listening to the muted sounds of London just stirring into life.

After a moment she became aware of a hand cupping her breast the thumb rubbing lightly over the nipple. Opening startled eyes, she saw Ryan, his face only inches away.

By the side of his mouth was a small crescent-shaped scar, a thin, silvery thread that disappeared into a shallow dimple when he smiled, as he was smiling at her now.

'Good morning. You're the only woman I know who wakes up beautiful.'

He himself looked fit and healthy, his tanned skin clear, his blue-violet eyes bright and, making him look very masculine and sexy, the beginnings of a dark stubble.

She could feel his breath, warm and fresh and sweet, on her lips, and she very much wanted him to kiss her.

As though reading her mind, he dipped his head and touched his mouth to hers. Without any urging, her lips parted beneath that light pressure.

With a little murmur of satisfaction, he deepened the kiss, while his hand began to travel over her slender body.

Her heart started to race and her breath quickened with pleasure as those experienced fingers reacquainted themselves with her slim waist, the curve of her hips, her flat stomach, the smooth skin of her inner thighs, and the nest of silky curls.

Feeling the swift leap of response, he broke the kiss and moved to nuzzle his face against the soft firmness of her breasts.

While she gasped and shuddered, he coaxed a dusky pink nipple into life with his tongue, before drawing it into his mouth and suckling sweetly.

By the time he had leisurely, and with great enjoyment, rediscovered each erogenous zone and had explored every inch of naked flesh, she was a quivering mass.

But, while giving her the greatest pleasure, he had skilfully kept her poised on the brink and, ignoring her husky pleas, had teased and tantalised without allowing her the satisfaction she craved.

She had imagined that her mind would stand apart, but when her body finally welcomed the weight of his, she was enslaved, heart and soul and mind. No part of her stood aloof while he took her to a climax of such intensity that she thought she might die.

Afterwards, her head on his shoulder, his body half supporting hers, she lay emotionally drained but completely fulfilled.

After a while, as though needing some final reassurance, Ryan asked quietly, 'Raynor was never your lover, was he?'

Unable to lie, she shook her head.

'But in two-and-a-half years there must have been others?'

'No.'

'No one?'

'No one.'

His sigh of relief was audible, before his arms tightened possessively and he said with soft triumph, 'My very own lollipop.'

Still entangled in a golden web of pleasure, she couldn't even summon up any resentment.

'Why was there no one else?' His sudden question took her by surprise.

Because he was the only man she had ever loved.

When she didn't answer, he persisted. 'You're young and lovely, and a passionate woman, so *why* was there no one else?'

Afraid that he might guess the truth and use it as a weapon against her, she asked, 'Have you never heard the old saying, once bitten, twice shy?'

'You make me sound like the big, bad wolf.' He spoke lightly, but she could have sworn that he was disappointed.

For a little while she lay, his breath stirring her hair, then she yawned, and a moment later, cradled close, she was asleep once more.

A light kiss awoke her. She opened her eyes to find Ryan sitting on the edge of the bed, freshly showered and shaved, and casually dressed.

He smelt pleasantly of shower gel, of male cologne and minty toothpaste.

'I hate having to disturb you when you were sleeping

like a babe, but breakfast will be here in a few minutes, and we really should get moving.'

Touching her cheek with a lean finger, he added, 'Which is a great pity. It would have been nice to have spent the morning in bed.'

His little reminiscent smile brought back vividly what had happened earlier and, recalling how she had begged and pleaded, her own sensual abandon, she blushed hotly.

As he rose to his feet, she stumbled out of bed and hightailed it for the bathroom, his soft, satisfied laugh following her.

How could she have surrendered control so easily? she asked herself vexedly, as she stripped the Cellophane from a toothbrush and cleaned her teeth with unnecessary vigour. She had been a weak fool! Where was her will-power, her pride?

But what use were self-recriminations? This was how it would always be with Ryan. Love, the emotional counterpart of sex, made her belong to him more than herself. When she had told Charles that it was Ryan she still loved, it had been the truth. She had never stopped loving him, and never would.

Despite the scented steam filling the shower stall, she shivered. It made her so vulnerable. Gave him such power to wound her. Power he would ruthlessly exploit.

Perhaps her only faint chance was to deny that love, to make him believe it was just physical attraction that drew her to him...

She was just finishing drying herself when a light knock at the bathroom door made her clutch the towel to her.

'Breakfast's arrived.'

'I'll only be a minute.' She was aware that she sounded breathless.

As soon as she was satisfied that he'd gone, she hurried into the bedroom and, opening her case, pulled out clean clothes and dressed as quickly as possible.

It was the same kind of neat, off-the-peg silk suit that Ryan had jeered at, but because she rarely went out socially there was little in her wardrobe other than business clothes.

Having made-up lightly, she was about to coil her abundance of ash-brown hair into its usual neat chignon when, recalling what had happened last time, she left it loose.

Ryan was standing by one of the windows in the sunny lounge looking out over the busy street to Kenelm Park. A breakfast trolley was waiting close by.

He turned at her approach and pulled out a chair for her with his customary politeness. When she was seated, he poured orange juice for them both and suggested, 'Bacon and scrambled eggs?'

'No thanks. Just toast and coffee.'

He watched her butter a piece of crisp golden toast before querying, 'So how did Raynor take it? I thought he might object to you selling yourself.'

She bit her lip before saying shortly, 'He did. In fact he was ready to tear up the cheque.'

'I presume you dissuaded him? Otherwise you wouldn't be here. I must say I'm rather relieved that he decided to put his own interests first.'

Hearing the faint hint of contempt in Ryan's voice, she flared. 'It wasn't like that at all. Don't sit there in judgement when you know nothing about it.'

Lifting those broad shoulders in a slight shrug, he asked, 'So how was it?'

'I had to lie through my teeth. I told him I *wanted* to come back to you.'

'And he bought it?'

'Not at first. He was still concerned that I was doing it for him.'

'So how did you manage to convince him otherwise?'

'I told him you had rung me at the gallery—Helen will confirm that—and, because I'd realised that marrying him would be a mistake, I'd agreed to come back to you, before I knew he had any problems.'

'It still sounds a bit thin.'

'In the end I was forced to tell him that I still loved you.'

'And do you?'

'You must be joking!'

His jaw tightened before he said coolly, 'I suppose it doesn't much matter how you feel so long as you're here.'

No, he wouldn't care a jot, she thought bitterly. But the fact that he didn't, still had the power to hurt her.

'Believe me, I wouldn't be here if there'd been any other way, but I couldn't stand by and see Charles totally ruined.'

'You don't think it was his own fault for being too reckless?'

'Charles is never reckless,' she said with certainty.

Ryan scowled, obviously annoyed by the way she was standing up for the other man. 'Well, you must admit that he was taking a serious risk, buying something that couldn't be fully authenticated.

'And, after all, it's unlikely that he's ever seen the genuine painting; and, if he has, he could only have been a child at the time. The painting has been in Otis Jefferson's private collection for the best part of thirty years.'

'Charles knows Roisser's work well, and he was convinced it was genuine. In the same circumstances plenty of men might have been tempted.'

'I wouldn't have thought that many would be so easily led astray.'

'Who are you to judge him? Have your business dealings always been whiter than white?'

She stopped speaking abruptly as a thought struck her. Charles had presumed that it had been *after* he had returned home and told her about *Footprints* being a worthless copy that she had mentioned it to Ryan... She had been right, Ryan must have known all along.

Her voice sharp, she asked, 'How did you find out about

all this? The whole thing was supposed to be a closely guarded secret, and you must have known what sort of mess Charles was going to be in before he did...'

Then, with a growing suspicion, she said, 'No, that isn't possible, unless—'

'I had second sight?' he suggested.

'But you haven't.'

'No, I haven't,' he agreed.

'So how did you know?' Only three people had been in on the deal. The seller—and he was hardly likely to have said anything—Charles himself, and Anderson, the man who had bought the forgery.

When Ryan hesitated, as if undecided whether or not to tell her, determined to get an answer, Virginia insisted, 'I want to know how you knew?'

Looking amused by her vehemence, he raised his hands in a gesture of surrender. 'Okay, I'll come clean.

'As you're aware, I've been on the lookout for some of your mother's earlier paintings, and I'd made arrangements to lunch with a man named Anderson, a collector-cum-dealer who has found stuff for me in the past.

'Having promised to keep an eye open for what I wanted, he hinted that if I was interested, so long as the deal was kept private, *Footprints* might possibly be for sale...

'I was interested, to say the least. You see, I happen to know the owner of *Footprints* well. Sir Humphrey Post is not only a friend of mine but he's also Beth's uncle...'

Though Virginia had known Beth was English, she still felt a shock of surprise, almost disbelief...

But Ryan was going on. 'Sir Humphrey stayed at the penthouse when he visited New York last year to buy *Footprints*. He said at the time that he'd bought the painting for his own private collection, and had no intention of ever parting with it...

'When I mentioned that small point to Anderson, he was more than a little upset, as he'd paid out for what he now felt convinced was a forgery... Though he admitted it was a clever piece of work, and he genuinely believed that Raynor had been taken in the same as he had...'

Virginia felt a pricking in her thumbs. Though Ryan's explanation was a perfectly logical one, somehow the whole thing sounded too pat, too much of a coincidence...

Yet what else could it possibly be?

After a moment, watching her face, Ryan continued casually, 'I presume you didn't see it?'

'No. I knew nothing about it until last night. But, even if I had, it wouldn't have made any difference. If Charles, who knows Roisser's work much better than I do, was fooled, I would have been too.'

'Don't underrate yourself. As well as a good eye, you have an instinct, a feel for paintings.'

'In this case I doubt if it would have worked. Though I've always wanted to see *Footprints*, I've only ever seen a copy.'

'If you'd still like to see the original, I'm quite sure Sir Humphrey would be happy to show it to you.'

Any other time Virginia would have jumped at the chance, but in the circumstances... Carefully, she began, 'I'd love to, but—'

'Then I'll ring and make arrangements for us to drop in at Ferndale Manor on our way to the airport.'

Built of mellow stone, with creeper-clad walls, mullioned windows, and twisted, barley-sugar chimneys, Ferndale Manor was a lovely old place.

It had in the past been secluded. But now, besieged by the present, its surrounding parkland had shrunk to a few acres, and new estates, both residential and industrial, a product of the airport, had sprung up around its perimeter.

Added to that, Sir Humphrey explained, after greeting both Ryan and Virginia warmly, the Manor was too close to the flight path for comfort.

'Still it makes getting hard of hearing a boon rather than a handicap.'

He was somewhere in his late seventies, she judged, a distinguished-looking man of medium height with silver hair and alert brown eyes.

Remembering Beth, she was struck at once by the family resemblance.

'I was very much hoping you could stay for lunch,' Sir Humphrey went on, 'but Ryan tells me you need to be at the airport before noon, so if you'd like to come this way?'

They crossed the long oak-panelled hall to a modern-looking door which, when unlocked, opened into a specially built, air-conditioned strongroom.

The walls were thickly lined, and every yard or so there was a shallow recess in which was hung a carefully lit painting.

Turning to Virginia, Sir Humphrey said, 'Would you like to take a quick look at the rest of my collection whilst you're here, my dear?'

'Please.' It was a chance she couldn't turn down.

The canvases, some by famous painters, others by lesser-known artists, were first class, she judged, and had been chosen with care.

'They're all picked from the point of view of personal liking, rather than as serious investments,' Sir Humphrey told her.

Then, showing he knew all about her, he asked shrewdly, 'What's your professional opinion?'

'As far as I'm concerned, art should be about enjoyment, but I imagine that, as serious investments, they're all a pretty safe bet.'

He nodded, smiling.

'Now for the one you specially wanted to see... Though, as *Footprints* hasn't yet been rehung, I'm afraid you won't be seeing it at its best,' he added as he led her to an easel and removed the cloth covering it.

Looking at the painting, Virginia could immediately see why it was regarded as one of Roisser's masterpieces.

It was both powerful and evocative. Not only was the brushwork brilliant, but the perspective seemed to draw the onlooker into the picture, making them part of it.

A snow scene, it depicted a narrow alleyway between overhanging half-timbered houses, deserted except for a woman clad in ankle-length, voluminous black, holding a small child by the hand. Their different sized footprints, dark against the crisp white layer, followed them along the uneven cobbles.

There was a sombre, almost tragic, feel to it.

In the bottom right-hand corner, black on white, was an elongated R.

'It's wonderful,' she breathed.

Sir Humphrey looked pleased. 'Yes, I've always thought so.'

As, scarcely listening, she continued to gaze at it enthralled, he added, 'It took me years to persuade Jefferson to part with it, and there's not many people who could have talked me into letting it out of my sight…'

Ryan made a sudden movement, breaking the spell. 'It's high time we were on our way, my love. Many thanks, Humphrey.'

When Virginia had added her thanks, the old man accompanied them back to the hall. As they said their goodbyes he took her hand with old-fashioned courtesy before clapping Ryan on the shoulder. 'I'm delighted to hear that congratulations are in order. Don't forget to invite me to the wedding.'

'We won't,' Ryan promised.

Feeling the way Virginia stiffened, he put an arm around her slim waist, and gave her a glinting, sidelong smile. 'We'll let you know the date as soon as we've had a chance to talk it over, won't we darling?'

So he was planning to carry on as if nothing had happened... Well she wouldn't be a party to it...

Sunshine glancing from its polished paintwork, the limousine was waiting on the apron with Maxwell at the wheel.

As soon as Ryan had helped Virginia in and had taken his place by her side, its tyres scrunching on the gravel, the sleek car pulled away.

Standing by the iron-studded oak door, shading his eyes with one hand and smiling genially, Sir Humphrey waved them off.

As they turned down the tree-lined drive, seeing that the glass panel between them and the chauffeur was open, Virginia bit her lip and said nothing, unwilling to go into battle with someone else listening.

Ryan's ironic glance told her he knew perfectly well what was on her mind, but was content to make her bide her time.

The drive to the airport, a comparatively short one, was made in silence. On arrival, Maxwell unloaded their small amount of luggage, and was thanked and tipped handsomely before they went through to a special sector.

As soon as the formalities had been completed, they were welcomed aboard the company jet.

Though full of inner agitation, Virginia had gone through the motions like someone trapped in a bad dream, who made no effort to escape because they knew there was no escape.

When Ryan had seen her settled in the plane's lounge and sipping a glass of fruit juice, he excused himself to go and have a word with the pilot.

After a short wait on the runway the plane took off, and had been airborne for some five minutes before he returned.

As soon as he got back there was a knock, and a white-coated steward wheeled in a luncheon trolley.

The meal was over and the trolley whisked away before

they were left alone and Virginia was able to give vent to her simmering anger.

As the door between the lounge and the galley slid into place, she rounded on Ryan, demanding, 'Why did you tell Sir Humphrey we were going to be married?'

'Did you want to keep it a secret?'

Gritting her teeth, she informed him, 'I've no intention of marrying you.'

'Backing out on the deal already?'

'You didn't say anything about us being married.'

'Surely you didn't think I was planning on just a short-term affair? No, I want what I've always wanted, marriage, and on a permanent basis.'

At the back of her mind had been the thought that if things became unbearable she could always run again. But if he was intent on a relationship she had always regarded as binding...

Watching her lose colour, he added sardonically, 'When I pay out that amount of money I expect a great deal in return... Not that merely having you in bed won't be worth every penny... But I happen to want a wife and family.'

A family... How could she agree to have Ryan's children when she knew he didn't love her?

Suddenly, despairingly, she said, 'I don't think I can bear it.'

His face changed. 'Surely it can't be that bad? Once you were happy to marry me.'

'That was when I thought—' she bit off the words, you loved me, and substituted '—you meant it to be a proper marriage.'

'Is there such a thing as an improper marriage?'

Unable to bear his levity, she covered her face with her hands. 'I don't want to marry you. It's bad enough having to go back to New York to face a family who hate me, and a woman who'll enjoy seeing me humiliated...'

He took her wrists and pulled her hands away from her

face, holding them in both of his. 'The family doesn't hate you. I'm sure you'll find that they're only too pleased to have you back...

'And as for Madeline, she's gone for good. Steven divorced her after she ran away with some second-rate film producer... He's been a different man since, so much happier...'

Just for a moment Virginia's spirits lifted, before common sense pointed out that, even if Madeline was no longer on the scene, it would make little difference to her relationship with Ryan.

Too much harm had already been done. If the family didn't hate her, *he* did.

Perhaps, as well as everything else, he blamed her for Madeline's departure, which might not have happened if she hadn't disrupted their plans.

Plans that still aroused a resentment so bitter that she wanted to strike out.

Tearing her hands free, she cried, 'Whether Madeline's there or not, I still couldn't bear to marry you. I don't want to be tied to a man who's capable of cuckolding his own stepbrother—'

Ryan's expression hardened. 'When we get back home I shall expect you to keep accusations like that to yourself, especially in front of Beth.'

Though quietly spoken, it was undoubtedly an order. Before she could attempt to challenge it, he added, 'I refuse to have her upset a second time.'

If only Ryan had cared for her the way he cared for Beth, and Madeline had never existed...

Suddenly feeling unutterably weary and defeated, Virginia sighed.

Picking up on that weariness, he asked in a more gentle tone, 'Tired?'

'A little,' she admitted.

'You didn't get much sleep last night.'

All her nights had been disturbed ones since Ryan had come back into her life, and the lack of proper rest was starting to tell.

'What about a siesta?' he suggested. 'A few hours sleep now will help enormously with the time difference.'

At the rear of the plane there was a bedroom with a luxurious double bed, and her pulse rate quickened as she wondered if he meant he was going too.

Apparently reading her thoughts, he said drily, 'I do mean *sleep*. I have some business to attend to.'

Flushing a little, she rose to her feet, telling herself how relieved she was. But in spite of everything the relief felt more like disappointment.

CHAPTER TEN

INDIGO eyes gleaming, he said, 'You look disappointed. If you are, I'm open to persuasion. Business can wait.'

Wondering how he could walk in and out of her mind as if it were his own penthouse, she said hardily, 'I'm not disappointed.'

'My sweet little liar.' Stepping closer, he rubbed the ball of his thumb across her lips, feeling them quiver beneath that light touch. 'You may not want to marry me, but you do want me...'

It was less than the truth. Despite her disillusionment, despite all her worries about what the future held, she longed for him, yearned for him, ached for him. And it was much more than merely physical. Her whole being was involved.

'And we've a lot of catching up to do.' His lips taking the place of his thumb, he kissed her. A thistledown caress that left her weak-kneed and trembling.

Sliding his hand inside her silk jacket so that it lay just over her heart, he said softly, 'And you can't hide it... I can feel your heart starting to race and your breathing getting faster, and if I touch you here...'

Reacting to his teasing caress, her nipple grew firm.

'Mmm...' he murmured, and began to undo the buttons of her blouse.

'Don't.' She pushed his hand away. 'Someone might come in.'

'Not without knocking. But if the thought bothers you, we could always go to bed.'

Well aware that he was as aroused as she was, Virginia was waiting for him to take her hand and lead her to the bedroom, when he said, 'Or perhaps you'd prefer to go alone, so you can sleep?'

Knowing that he had purposely left the ball in her court and unwilling to let him have the satisfaction of crowing, her voice as dismissive as she could make it, she said, 'Yes, I would.'

'Then, so you shall.'

She should have been warned by his steely smooth tone. Instead, believing she'd won, she turned and headed for the bedroom.

'But first, so you'll be able to sleep...'

He had followed her noiselessly and, before she could begin to guess what he intended, he'd spun her round and backed her up against the dividing wall.

Leaning his body weight forward, so she was pressed against the smoothness of the bulkhead, he used one hand to free her breast from the confines of her bra, while the other slid up her nylon-clad thigh, past the lacy top of her stocking to the edge of her dainty briefs.

'Please,' she begged.

His answer to her plea was a wolfish smile, and a moment later his mouth was at her breast and his long fingers were wreaking havoc. He wasn't satisfied until he'd turned her into a shuddering mass of sensations.

When he finally released her and moved back, eyes still closed, she staggered, and he was forced to steady her.

A hand beneath her elbow, he steered her through the bulkhead door and into the bedroom.

Pulling the blind down over the window, he said, 'Get a good sleep so you'll be nice and fresh when we reach New York.'

His voice was condescending, the mockery blatant.

She adjusted her bra and pulled her gaping blouse together before charging thickly, 'You're a swine.'

He pretended to look hurt. 'I didn't expect to be reviled.

In fact, as I've eased your frustration at the expense of my own, I thought you might want to thank me.'

Knowing perfectly well that Ryan's usual approach was a great deal more subtle and sensitive, and it had been done simply to prove a point, she said furiously, 'Go to hell! You only meant to punish and degrade me. You're cruel and sadistic...'

His mouth tightened as though he were in pain. 'If I am, it's what you've made me—'

A knock cut through his words.

Blocking the bedroom door, Ryan called, 'Yes, what is it?'

A man's voice queried, 'Can you spare just a moment, Mr Falconer?'

'I'll be right there.'

Turning to Virginia, he took her shoulders and stood looking down at her, a strange, bleak expression on his face. Then bending his dark head he gave her a brief but punitive kiss.

A second later he was gone.

Sinking down on the bed she stared blindly after him until, reaction setting in, she began to tremble violently.

What had he meant by, 'If I am it's what you've made me...?' He'd looked so bitter, so wretched, angry with both himself and her...

After a minute or two, making an effort to control her shaking limbs, she took off her suit and blouse and crawled beneath the duvet.

She fell asleep almost as soon as her head touched the pillow, and she only awakened when the plane began its descent and Ryan knocked with a refreshing cup of tea.

If he had seemed himself she might have tried to talk to him, but he looked aloof and unapproachable, and left with just the curt warning. 'We'll be landing in about fifteen minutes.'

When they reached JFK, as though fate was having a

cruel little joke at her expense, the same car and the same chauffeur as last time were waiting.

She found that New York was hot and sunny and heartbreakingly familiar as they repeated the drive into the city. The only difference was that this time it was made in silence as Ryan, his dark face sombre, a devil riding on his shoulder, stared into space.

Remembering the joy of her first visit, and contrasting it with her feelings now, by the time the car stopped outside Falconer's Tower, Virginia was a mass of nerves.

With the kind of irony she might have expected, they were even greeted by the same security man, who beamed at them, and said, 'Afternoon Mr Falconer. Nice to see you back, Miss Adams.'

'Thank you, George.' She managed to return his smile.

Ryan led the way to the elevator, and they rode up in silence, standing apart and avoiding contact, like two wary strangers.

When they reached the top foyer, to Virginia's surprise, Ryan opened the door of what had once been her apartment, and ushered her inside.

'I presume that until we get things sorted out you would prefer to be here rather than the penthouse?'

'Y-yes, thank you,' she stammered.

Sunny and spacious, it was just as she remembered it, and brought a swift rush of memories that threatened to engulf her.

Dropping the key into her palm, he said coolly, 'Beth asked if you would pop down and see her as soon as you're settled?'

Virginia swallowed hard. 'Of course.'

Sounding a little more human, he told her, 'There's no need to look so worried. You won't have to face them all. Janice is in Washington for the weekend, and Steven is on holiday with his new girlfriend, so Beth is on her own.'

Needing to get it over, Virginia said, 'I'll go down

straight away. There's only one thing... What am I going to tell her?'

He raised a dark brow. 'About what?'

'She's bound to ask why I left so suddenly.'

'And you hesitate to damn me in her eyes?' Then, caustically, he added, 'I'm surprised you care.'

'If I hadn't cared about tearing the family apart, I would have told her *then* exactly what Madeline had told me,' Virginia said quietly.

'It's a great pity you didn't. The whole thing was a tissue of lies, and Beth would have known it.'

As Virginia stared at him, shaken by the unmistakable ring of truth in his voice, he said, 'When you do go down I'd like you to wear this...'

He felt in his pocket and produced a ring, which he slipped onto her engagement finger.

'I had intended to give it to you earlier, but...' With a slight shrug he allowed the words to tail off.

Like someone in a dream she found herself gazing down at the sardonyx. So he had kept it all this time...

As he turned away, tears threatening, she begged, 'Please, Ryan... Won't you come with me?'

'I think this is something you should do alone. Woman to woman, so to speak.'

'But I don't know what to say to her... What to tell her... Suppose she asks *why* I came back to you?'

His chiselled mouth twisted in the semblance of a smile. 'Try the truth. In many ways Beth's a lot tougher than she appears.'

Watching him walk away, and knowing he was going to give her no further help, she hesitated. Then, annoyed by her own cowardice, she squared her shoulders and made her way downstairs.

Beth answered the door and, after one glance at her visitor's face, held out her arms.

Being enfolded in a warm hug of welcome, broke the tension and allowed Virginia's tears to brim over.

After a moment she drew back and, fumbling in her pocket, produced a tissue and blew her nose. 'I'm sorry.'

Her brown eyes suspiciously bright, Beth said, 'You've no need to be sorry for anything.'

Then briskly, she said, 'Now there's someone waiting to see you…' Leading the way to the living-room, she opened the door, adding, 'And so you can speak quite frankly, I'm going to wait in the kitchen.'

Madeline, who had been sitting on the couch, rose to her feet. Beautifully dressed, her blonde hair expertly styled, she looked her usual glamorous self.

Reading Virginia's shocked expression correctly, she said, 'No, this wasn't my idea.'

Then, with more than a touch of venom, she said, 'I need to be on set first thing tomorrow morning, but my ex-mother-in-law insisted on me coming all the way over here.'

All at once icy cool and composed, Virginia said, 'She must have a reason.'

'Oh, she has. She wants me to tell you the truth about what happened between Ryan and myself…'

'I already know,' Virginia told her calmly. 'You had an affair. An affair that ended *before* you married Steven. But because you were jealous, and didn't want Ryan to marry me, you told me a pack of lies.'

'Which you were fool enough to believe.' Madeline's voice held swingeing contempt. 'If it had been *me* Ryan was going to marry, I wouldn't have given up so easily. But then, I *wanted* him. Which you obviously didn't, or you would have fought for him. It's a great pity he's so obsessed with you. You don't deserve him.'

Turning on her heel, she headed for the door. When she reached it, she said over her shoulder, 'If that interfering old bat was expecting me to kowtow and say how sorry I am, she'll be disappointed.'

A second later the door slammed shut behind her.

When she had had a moment to gather herself, Virginia made her way through to the kitchen on legs that weren't quite steady.

Beth looked up from pouring tea. 'I thought I heard her go.' Then, anxiously, she added, 'You look a bit pale. Are you all right?'

'Fine,' Virginia said, with more determination than accuracy. Sitting down at the table, she accepted a cup of tea, and sipped gratefully.

'Perhaps I shouldn't have sprung it on you like that,' Beth admitted. 'But there was so little time and, as she was the one who had caused all the trouble in the first place, I thought it was best if you heard the truth from *her*.'

'How did you persuade her to come…? It was you?'

'Yes, Ryan knows nothing about it… He might be very angry when he finds out. But I felt I must do something. In many ways, he's my favourite son, and he's been so dreadfully unhappy…'

Her eyes filled with tears. Blinking them away, she went on doggedly, 'And "persuade" is hardly the right word. *Coerce* is closer to the truth.'

Smiling now at Virginia's expression, she went on, 'I'd better tell you the whole story. Some time ago I found out, quite by chance, that Madeline was having an affair with a man named Christian Gent, a Hollywood film producer.

'He'd come to New York to try to get backing for his latest film, *Persephone*, but after his last two had been complete flops he was finding it practically impossible.

'It was when I discovered he'd promised Madeline the starring role, which she was dead keen to have, that I decided to take a hand. She'd been making Steven so miserable that I couldn't bear it any longer. I offered to put up a large sum of money in secret if she would consent to leave New York for good and let Steven divorce her.

'As well as giving her the part, apparently Gent wanted to marry her, so she was only too happy to agree. I hope and believe it's been for the best.'

'I'm sure it has,' Virginia reassured her. 'Ryan said how much happier Steven has been since Madeline left.'

Beth smiled her relief. 'I must admit I haven't dared tell either of them. Though I may have to if *Persephone* proves to be a great success and the money starts rolling in…

'Judging by Christian Gent's past record, it's hardly likely, but if I lose every penny I've put into it, it will still have been well worth it.'

After a moment, harking back, Virginia said, 'You were going to tell me how you coerced Madeline into coming here?'

The older woman gave an impish grin. 'Simple. To make sure she toed the line, I'd arranged to have the money paid over in four installments, so all I had to do was threaten to withhold the final one if she didn't do as I asked.'

Virginia was impressed by the martial spirit of a woman she had regarded as too meek and gentle for her own good.

Hesitantly, she began, 'There's one thing I'd like to ask you… How did you know Madeline had caused all the trouble?'

'I didn't know for sure until a couple of days ago when Ryan came home saying he needed to talk to me. He told me everything he'd learnt, and I admitted that, like him, I'd always suspected Madeline of being at the bottom of it.

'He was *livid*. It's just as well she wasn't still here or I don't know what might have happened.'

She sighed. 'I only wish you'd talked to me at the time instead of just running…'

'I wish I had,' Virginia said in a heartfelt voice, 'but I was afraid to in case—' She broke off.

'In case I believed all that rubbish? Oh, my dear, I know

Ryan too well to credit for one instant that he would have played around with Steven's wife...'

Virginia drew a deep, gasping breath of pain. Beth's absolute certainty was like a dagger through the heart. If only she had had that kind of faith...

'Apart from anything else,' Beth went on, 'he absolutely *adored* you, and I've always known that when Ryan fell in love he would be a one-woman man.'

On the rack, Virginia whispered, 'None of this would have happened if I'd trusted him.'

'Perhaps, as events moved so quickly, you didn't know him well enough. But now...well, you have a lifetime ahead of you...'

Seeing Virginia's tortured expression, Beth asked with sudden anxiety, 'It is all right, isn't it? You're wearing his ring again, and you do still love him, don't you?'

'Yes, I still love him. Even when I believed the worst, I never stopped loving him.'

'Then, try telling him so.'

'It's too late. He doesn't love me any longer. All he wants is revenge. He hates me for leaving him the way I did.'

Beth shook her head. 'Though he was hurt and bitterly disappointed that you hadn't trusted him, I'm quite certain he still loves you.

'Off you go now and talk to him. Don't mention that Madeline was here unless you're forced.'

'I won't,' Virginia promised.

The two women hugged each other briefly.

Virginia had been having a struggle to hold back the flood of emotion that threatened to engulf her, and before she reached the stairs she was weeping.

Knowing she couldn't face Ryan until she had herself under control, she headed for her own door and, blinded by tears, stumbled inside.

If only she hadn't allowed Madeline to do such mischief...

But what was the use of blaming Madeline? It was her own doing. *She* was the one who, through lack of trust, had caused both Ryan and herself so much pain.

As Beth had said, she hadn't really *known* him, and remembering how, when she'd called him cruel and sadistic, he'd said, 'If I am, it's what you've made me...' she felt as though she were bleeding to death.

Giving way to the anguish that filled her, she sank onto the living-room couch and began to sob, deep wrenching sobs that hurt her throat and took more breath than she'd got.

'For goodness' sake, don't cry like that,' Ryan said harshly.

Startled, she lifted a ravaged face to see him standing in the doorway.

'The door wasn't properly closed, so I walked in. I'll go if you want me to.'

It was too late. She shook her head.

He frowned. 'Surely Beth hasn't...?'

'No, Beth's been wonderful...' But as though the floodgates had opened, the tears were still flowing, pouring down her cheeks in tracks of shiny wetness, the sobs still rising in her throat.

With a sound almost like a groan he moved to the couch and, sitting down by her side, took her in his arms. Cradling her head to his chest, his mouth muffled against her silky hair, he rocked her a little, as though she was a child.

'I'm sorry for the way I've treated you...I've behaved like a swine...'

Full of guilt as she was, his apology only made her cry harder.

Murmuring inarticulate words of comfort, and still cuddling her closely, he let her cry herself out.

When the sobs finally gave way to sniffs and hiccups,

he took a handkerchief from his pocket and, holding her away a little, dried her face.

Taking the handkerchief from him, she blew her nose and said with a kind of pathetic dignity, 'I'm sorry. I shouldn't have given way like that. I must look an awful mess.'

Glancing at her pink nose and swollen eyes, her blotched cheeks, he shook his head. 'You look beautiful.'

She made a sound, a cross between a laugh and a sob, and one last tear rolled down her cheek.

He caught it with his thumb and put it in his mouth. 'Don't cry any more. It'll be all right. I promise.'

'Will it?' she asked thickly.

'I shouldn't have tried to make you come back to me when you so obviously hated the idea. You can go home as soon as you like.'

It was the last thing she had expected to hear. Blankly, she said, 'I don't understand.'

He repeated his words.

'What about Charles?'

'Don't worry, I've no intention of demanding my money back.'

'No, we made a deal.'

Sighing, he admitted, 'It wasn't fair.'

'It was more than fair, generous even, and I agreed to it.'

'Being the kind of woman you are, you had little option. But, when I say it wasn't fair, I mean exactly that. What I told you previously was a complete fabrication. I engineered the whole thing.'

As she stared at him open-mouthed, he explained, '"Mr Smith," who turned out to be quite a good actor, was working for me—'

'*You* sold Charles the forgery?'

'No, I sold him the real thing.'

All at once, she recalled Sir Humphrey saying, '*Foot-*

prints hasn't yet been rehung.' Then, though it had scarcely registered at the time, 'There's not many people who could have talked me into letting it out of my sight...'

'You borrowed it from Sir Humphrey!'

'Not exactly. Beth did. And before you condemn her, she did it in the desperate hope that it would bring the two of us together, and everything would be all right.'

But everything wasn't all right...

Pushing away that thought, Virginia said jerkily, 'I don't see how you managed it.'

'"Anderson" was also working for me. Posing as a collector who wasn't over-scrupulous, he had previously contacted Raynor and made his interest in Roisser's works known.

'As soon as Raynor was hooked, confident that he had a buyer, he got in touch with New Finance—one of my financial associates—who had recently offered him a short-term loan on favourable terms. I immediately gave them a cheque to cover that loan.

'Once Anderson had "bought" the painting and Raynor had his money back, plus a handsome profit, if you'd shown any sign of coming back to me, I would have left it at that. But when you were so adamant that you were going to marry him, I was forced to go on.

'The minute Anderson cried forgery, Raynor panicked. As I'd expected, he checked with Jefferson as well as Sir Humphrey.

'After Sir Humphrey had assured him that *he* owned *Footprints* and invited him to go and see the painting, the one thing Raynor failed to do was try to reclaim what he now regarded as a worthless copy.

'By the time he reached Ferndale Manor, the authenticated painting was there for him to see...'

She shivered. Ryan must have wanted revenge very badly to have gone to so much trouble.

Curiously, she asked, 'What would you have done if I'd refused to play ball?'

'I would have told Raynor the truth. But, being the kind of woman you are, I thought it was a pretty safe bet.'

Bleakly, she said, 'All that, just to force me to come back to you.'

'*Force* is the operative word. I should have had the sense to see that it wouldn't work.'

He sighed deeply. 'But I can't bear to see you this unhappy. As soon as you feel ready to travel I'll take you back to London.'

If it had been just revenge he'd wanted, he wouldn't have cared how unhappy she was.

Remembering Beth's certainty that he still loved her, Virginia gathered her courage and said, 'I don't want to go back to London.'

'Well, if you prefer to stay in New York I'll buy you an apartment and—'

'I've got an apartment... Though I'd much prefer to live in a penthouse.'

'You don't have to stay with me just because we made a bargain—'

'I don't *have* to stay with you,' she agreed, 'I happen to *want* to.'

He shook his head. 'I can't bear to see you so utterly wretched...'

'I was only wretched because I'd made such a mess of things.' Then in growing desperation, she said, 'Please, Ryan, I love you. I've never stopped loving you, and I do want to marry you.'

'I've done a lot of thinking in the past few hours, and it wouldn't work. Marriage should be built on *trust* as well as love.'

She bit her lip until she tasted blood. 'Not trusting you is something I bitterly regret... Perhaps, as Beth says, I didn't know you well enough. But what Madeline told me sounded so plausible... And she was so beautiful...'

'She was a first-class bitch,' he said shortly. 'Unfortunately it took me a while to realise it. I knew from the first that she was a gold-digger but as you say, she was beautiful, and I could afford her.

'The trouble started when I quickly grew tired of her and wanted to pay her off. It seems she'd set her sights on marriage, and when I made it plain that I had no intention of marrying her, determined to get a rich husband, she transferred her attention to Steven.

'I tried to warn the poor devil, but he was completely infatuated, and dead set on marrying her. When I persisted, he thought it was just jealousy on my part. Though none of us liked it, for the sake of family harmony, we did our best to accept the situation.

'But hell hath no fury, and all that, and when Madeline saw a chance to get back at me, she took it.' Grimly, he added, 'It's just as well I didn't know at the time or I might have been tempted to throttle her...'

'But Madeline wasn't solely to blame,' Virginia said sadly. 'It was as much my fault for believing her.'

'Why did you?'

She tried to explain. 'Perhaps it wasn't so much lack of trust in you, as lack of faith in myself. No one had ever loved me...'

His hard face softened.

'And right from the start I couldn't imagine why you were bothering with someone as ordinary as me. It didn't make sense that you would go to so much trouble simply to find an assistant curator, and I was half convinced that your interest had something to do with my parents. Even when you proposed, I could hardly credit that you, who could have anyone, would want to marry me...

'And though I'd fallen in love with you at first sight, I

found it almost impossible to believe you had fallen in love with me. It all seemed too sudden...'

'Whereas it wasn't sudden at all. I loved you before we even met.'

Wide eyes on his face, she said, 'But that's not possible.'

'Let me show you something.'

Taking her hand he led her out of the apartment, across the foyer, and into the penthouse.

Hanging in the living-room was a painting she had never seen before.

It was a fairly small oil-on-canvas portrait of a girl with long ash-brown hair curling onto her shoulders. She was sitting on a wooden stool looking through a rain-misted window, drops running down the glass like tears.

Her thin body, clad in a simple pink cotton shift, had a dejected droop, and her lovely face, seen in profile, was melancholy. There was a sense of rejection, of sadness, of inner loneliness.

Yet coupled with that was a feeling of expectancy, as if at any moment a loved one might appear and that wistful young face would smile, the body become eager and welcoming.

As Virginia stared at it speechlessly, Ryan said, 'I first saw *Wednesday's Child* about three years ago when I was putting on an exhibition of your mother's work at the gallery.

'She gave me permission to go into her studio and look through some of her paintings that had never previously been exhibited.

'*Wednesday's Child* had been wrapped in hessian and left behind a stack of old canvases, and I came across it by accident.

'From the word go I was bewitched, enchanted. I couldn't take my eyes off it. If it's possible to fall in love with a picture, then that's what I did.

'I imagined myself as being the one that young girl was

waiting for, the one who would replace her sense of rejection and sadness with warmth and happiness.

'It took a lot of subtle pressure before your mother finally, and with the greatest reluctance, admitted who the girl was.

'When I asked if I could buy the painting, she replied that it wasn't for sale, and she flatly refused to have it exhibited.

'It's my belief that she hadn't been able to destroy something she knew was good, but she'd kept *Wednesday's Child* hidden away because it was too revealing. It showed too clearly how she'd failed as a mother, and maybe she felt ashamed.

'It was several weeks before I could get her to talk about you, but when I finally learnt where you were and what you were doing I couldn't rest until I'd seen for myself what you were really like.

'You were even more beautiful than your portrait, and it was instant enchantment all over again...'

She lifted a glowing face. 'Then, you really *did* fall in love with me?'

'Madly.'

'Beth thinks you still love me.'

'Does she?' he asked drily. 'What do you think?'

Her confidence suddenly shaken, she said, 'I don't know.'

He sighed. 'Tell me what I need to say or do to finally convince you?'

She moved closer and put her hands, flat-palmed, against his chest. 'Say, stay with me... Say, marry me... Then take me to bed.'

'Are you sure that's what you want?'

'I'm sure.'

Taking her hands, he raised them to his lips. 'Stay with me... Marry me... Never leave me again.'

'I won't,' she promised.

Sweeping her into his arms he carried her through to the bedroom.

Their lovemaking was fervent and rapturous, with the added dimension of love not only felt, but declared.

When their hunger for each other was temporarily appeased, and they lay closely entwined, Virginia asked, 'How come you've got *Wednesday's Child*? You said Mother wouldn't part with it.'

'After you ran away, I went to see your parents hoping they might have some idea where you were, but though they were sympathetic, they couldn't help.

'Two days later, *Wednesday's Child* turned up at the penthouse. A gift from your mother.

'So you already had it when you asked Charles if he could get it... In other words, you only mentioned it to rattle me...'

Kissing her ear, he asked, 'Did I succeed?'

'Yes.' She shivered. 'You frightened me half to death with all that talk of revenge.'

'And that's just what it was, talk. I wanted you back, but my pride wouldn't allow me to plead.

'I thought once we were together again and things had settled down I'd tell you the truth. Tell you how much I loved you.'

'Go ahead,' she invited.

He traced her cheek with his finger. 'I've already told you.'

Nestling closer, she said wistfully, 'I wouldn't mind hearing it again.'

'I love you more than words can say and, if you can stand it, I'll tell you so every day for the rest of our lives.'

'Try me.'

His indigo eyes adoring, he laughed, and kissed her. 'I might just do that.'

Modern Romance™
...seduction and
passion guaranteed

Tender Romance™
...love affairs that
last a lifetime

Sensual Romance™
...sassy, sexy and
seductive

Blaze
...sultry days and
steamy nights

Medical Romance™
...medical drama on
the pulse

Historical Romance™
...rich, vivid and
passionate

29 new titles every month.

*With all kinds of Romance for
every kind of mood...*

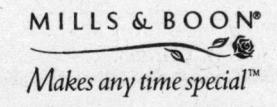

MILLS & BOON®

Makes any time special™

MAT4

MILLS & BOON

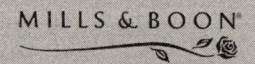

Modern Romance™

THE SHEIKH'S CHOSEN WIFE by Michelle Reid

Leona misses her arrogant, passionate husband very much – but there is little point in staying when she's failed to deliver the son and heir he needed. When Hassan tricks her into returning to him, Leona is puzzled. Why does he want her at his side once again?

THE BLACKMAIL BABY by Penny Jordan

A shocking revelation on Imogen's wedding day made her run right out of her brand-new husband's life. She thought she would never see Dracco Barrington again – but four years later Imogen needs money, and super-rich Dracco makes an outrageous proposal...

THE PREGNANT MISTRESS by Sandra Marton

Greek tycoon Demetrios Karas is in danger of blowing a whole business deal if he doesn't make his translator, Samantha Brewster, his mistress. Demetrios suspects they are made for each other in the bedroom. Now he just has to persuade Samantha!

TO MARRY McKENZIE by Carole Mortimer

When Logan McKenzie learned that his mother was to marry for the third time, he discovered that Darcy, his very pretty stepsister-to-be, was in danger of being hurt by this marriage. He immediately found himself getting very involved...

On sale 5th April 2002

Available at most branches of WH Smith, Tesco, Martins, Borders, Eason, Sainsbury's and most good paperback bookshops.

MILLS & BOON

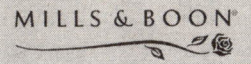

Modern Romance™

WOLFE'S TEMPTRESS by Robyn Donald

Rowan was charming, with an irresistible beauty and an innocence that took Wolfe Talamantes by surprise. The combination was beguiling, and they fell into bed at first sight. Then Rowan fled. But Wolfe had found her once – he'd find her again...

A SHOCKING PASSION by Amanda Browning

Good looks and sophisticated charm have always been Ellie's downfall, and the moment she sets eyes on the irresistible Jack Thornton all reason disappears! Jack is set on skilful seduction and Ellie is determined to resist. But one taste of intoxicating passion and she knows she wants more...

THE BILLIONAIRE IS BACK by Myrna Mackenzie

After convincing herself that she doesn't need a man in her life, Helena meets Jackson Castle. The attraction is instantaneous, but Helena's conspicuous pregnancy is a constant reminder that passion has a price...

THE MILLIONAIRE'S WAITRESS WIFE by Carolyn Zane

Millionaire Dakota Brubaker found it refreshing that his sassy waitress mistook him for a regular guy. But just as he was about to ask Elizabeth out, she proposed to him! She urgently needed a working class groom to shock her interfering family. Could Dakota keep his millions secret?

On sale 5th April 2002

Available at most branches of WH Smith, Tesco, Martins, Borders, Eason, Sainsbury's and most good paperback bookshops.

FREE
2 BOOKS
AND A SURPRISE GIFT!

We would like to take this opportunity to thank you for reading this Mills & Boon® book by offering you the chance to take TWO more specially selected titles from the Modern Romance™ series absolutely FREE! We're also making this offer to introduce you to the benefits of the Reader Service™ —

- ★ FREE home delivery
- ★ FREE monthly Newsletter
- ★ FREE gifts and competitions
- ★ Exclusive Reader Service discount
- ★ Books available before they're in the shops

Accepting these FREE books and gift places you under no obligation to buy; you may cancel at any time, even after receiving your free shipment. Simply complete your details below and return the entire page to the address below. ***You don't even need a stamp!***

YES! Please send me 2 free Modern Romance™ books and a surprise gift. I understand that unless you hear from me, I will receive 4 superb new titles every month for just £2.55 each, postage and packing free. I am under no obligation to purchase any books and may cancel my subscription at any time. The free books and gift will be mine to keep in any case.

P2ZEC

Ms/Mrs/Miss/Mr .... Initials ....

BLOCK CAPITALS PLEASE

Surname ....

Address ....

....

.... Postcode ....

Send this whole page to:
UK: FREEPOST CN81, Croydon, CR9 3WZ
EIRE: PO Box 4546, Kilcock, County Kildare (stamp required)

Offer valid in UK and Eire only and not available to current Reader Service subscribers to this series. We reserve the right to refuse an application and applicants must be aged 18 years or over. Only one application per household. Terms and prices subject to change without notice. Offer expires 30th June 2002. As a result of this application, you may receive offers from other carefully selected companies. If you would prefer not to share in this opportunity please write to The Data Manager at the address above.

Mills & Boon® is a registered trademark owned by Harlequin Mills & Boon Limited.
Modern Romance™ is being used as a trademark.